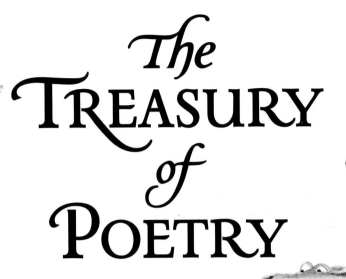

The TREASURY of POETRY for CHILDREN

With a foreword by
CHARLES CAUSLEY

Illustrated by
DIZ WALLIS

Selection edited by
SUSIE GIBBS

BARNES
&NOBLE
BOOKS
NEW YORK

BARNES
&NOBLE
BOOKS
NEW YORK

First published in Great Britain 1997 by Macmillan Children's Books
a division of Macmillan Publishers Limited
25 Eccleston Place, London SW1W 9NF
and Basingstoke

Associated companies throughout the world

ISBN 0 760707545

A CIP catalogue record for this book is available from the British Library.

Colour reproduction by Speedscan Ltd
Typeset by Intype, London
Printed and bound in Italy

Contents

WILD AND FREE

'Sharing the sunlight with the free'

PETS AND FRIENDS

'You own the freedom we have lost'

WEIRD AND WONDERFUL

'Moonlight, summer moonlight'

HILL AND DALE

'O, wild birds, come and nest in me!'

FOOD AND FUN

BALLADS AND STORIES

'And people call me the Pied Piper'

HOPES AND DREAMS

'Oh, to be an eagle'

STUFF AND NONSENSE

'Sssnnnwhuffffll?'

RIVER AND SEA

'The tide in the river runs deep'

YOUNG AND OLD

'I remember, I remember'

HEROES AND WARRIORS

'Dim drums throbbing, in the hills half heard'

LOVE AND FRIENDSHIP

'A frog he would a wooing go'

ODDS AND ENDS

'The Wraggle Taggle Gypsies, O!'

GOOD NIGHT

'Sunset and evening star'

Foreword

WHAT do we mean by the phrase 'poetry for children'? For me W. H. Auden, writing of the work of the great Walter de la Mare[1], answered this question once and for all. 'It must never be forgotten,' he said, 'that, while there are some good poems which are only for adults, because they pre-suppose adult experience in their readers, there are no good poems which are only for children.'

I remember wondering, in my earliest years as a primary school teacher, why my so-called 'poetry' lessons invariably fell flat, although made up of what I believed to be perfectly acceptable 'children's' verse of the day: simple songs and jingles, light verses about animals, comic tales of those who were judged to be 'characters', and the like. All these offerings were accepted politely by my captive audiences, though clearly without much enthusiasm. Shamefully, I had failed to remember the excellent advice of a wise and experienced tutor. 'Never forget,' he had said. 'Feed the lambs.'

Then, one lucky day, I arrived before one of my classes with the wrong set of books, only one of which was of poetry: a newly-acquired selection of English and Scottish traditional ballads made by Robert Graves. I'd had no time to study it properly, and retreat was out of the question. I opened the book and began to read.

Young Beichan he was a noble lord
And a peer of high degree;
He hath taken ship at London Town,
For that Christ's Tomb he would see.

He sailèd west, and he sailèd east
Till he came to Galilee,
Where he was cast in prison strong
And handled cruelly.[2]

At this point, out of sheer nerves, I muddled a turn of the pages. In the small silence while I put things right, I was startled by a boy's voice from the middle of the class. '*Go on, then!*' And I knew that, at last, I'd secured a genuine audience, if only of one. I also knew that perhaps, as far as my work as a teacher was concerned, I'd discovered one key to the world of poetry for children.

Beginning in this simple fashion, it became increasingly clear to me that given a little trust and encouragement, children are as capable of interpreting the signs and signals, the secret messages of poetry, as adults are venturesome enough to make available to them. It was Sir John Betjeman who defined such secret messages with wonderful simplicity as 'tones of meaning beyond the surface one'.

Few children in this or any other age can be entirely unfamiliar with the ancient patterns of birth, love, marriage, infidelity, betrayal, sickness, old age, death. All these elements form part of the fabric of our early popular poetry, presented in a simple-seeming and undidactic manner as it reflects the ways of the world.

Who can resist a tale well told? The ballad moves with breathtaking speed and clarity (no excess of words here), the narrative leaping forward from stanza to stanza like the images in a film. The total absence of sentimentality, the lack of moralising on the part of the narrator, are all essentials in this plainly-spoken form that, with its sturdy companion the folk-song, have held their places securely in our culture over the centuries. 'The young are a secret society,' said the Czech novelist and playwright Karel Capek, 'and the old have forgotten that they once belonged to it.' It's the business, surely then, of those of us no longer children, to try to remember.

A poet, of course, is not obliged to make a poem, whatever its form, entirely accessible at a first reading. A poem, by its nature, may hold certain qualities in reserve. It may not burn itself out, so to speak, in one brilliant flash of light. A poem is a living organism, capable of continuous development and the most subtle of changes. It may contain both a revelation and a mystery. We need to be aware not only of what is said, but also of what the poet most carefully has left unsaid.

If we take poems to pieces and put them together again, unlike pieces of machinery they may give no reason why they 'work', nor are they obliged to do so. A poem has no single 'meaning'. This may differ with each reader, who interprets the piece in accordance with his or her own age, experience and sensibility. However many times we read a poem, no matter how seemingly familiar the text, it is perfectly capable of revealing some fresh quality, some resonance hitherto unnoticed in the course of a hundred earlier readings. And we should neither discount nor ignore the powerful effect of the sound of verse, and allow – with patience – 'understanding' to declare itself in its own good time. Meanwhile, we may share with Coleridge the mysterious music of *Kubla Khan* (page 106).

> *Weave a circle round him thrice,*
> *And close your eyes with holy dread,*
> *For he on honey-dew hath fed,*
> *And drunk the milk of paradise.*

I have always believed there to be something magical about a well-made poem. The Spanish poet Federico García Lorca said that a poem emits what he described as *sonidos negros*: black sounds. Such sounds, he said, accompany the best of art, whether it is in words or music, paint or stone.

Poems are not word games. The writing of poetry is an activity in which words are put out to work, not to grass. When writing the poem (often a slow and intensely arduous process) the poet is careful to allow a space, invisible to the bare eye, which may be engaged by the mind and imagination of the reader. Not that the poet is conscious of his or her audience when writing. At that time the poet is both writer and reader, and the poem is for the poet alone. And is it a function of poetry to provide us with 'answers'? I think it is the more difficult one of asking questions.

Unsurprisingly, the beautiful word 'anthology' is Greek in origin: 'a collection of flowers'. Such gatherings of flowers of verse have a history reaching as far back as the first century BC with *The Garland of Meleager*, made by the Greek poet of that name. Then, as now, every anthologist must hope that the choices made may result in new discoveries on the part of the reader and a wider acquaintance with the work of individual poets. I would also hope that this, in turn, may lead to the making by the reader of perhaps the finest and most companionable of all anthologies: one entirely personal and private. The world of words is wide, its prospects boundless. As Sylvia Plath writes in her poem *Mushrooms* (page 32):

> *We shall by morning*
> *Inherit the earth.*
> *Our foot's in the door.*

Charles Causley
Launceston, Cornwall, 1997

1 *A Choice of de la Mare's Verse* (selected by W. H. Auden, Faber 1963)
2 *Young Beichan*, Anon., page 156

BEGINNINGS

'When the sun rises'

When the sun rises

When the sun rises, I go to work,
When the sun goes down, I take my rest,
I dig the well from which I drink,
I farm the soil that yields my food,
I share creation, Kings can do no more.

Anon. (Chinese, 2500 BC)

March

Dear March – Come In –
How glad I am –
I hoped for you before –
Put down your Hat –
You must have walked –
How out of Breath you are –
Dear March, how are you, and the Rest –
Did you leave Nature well –
Oh March, Come right up stairs with me –
I have so much to tell –

I got your Letter, and the Birds –
The Maples never knew that you were coming –
   till I called
I declare – how Red their Faces grew –
But March, forgive me – and
All those Hills you left for me to Hue –
There was no Purple suitable –
You took it all with you –

Who knocks? That April.
Lock the Door –
I will not be pursued –
He stayed away a Year to call
When I am occupied –
But trifles look so trivial
As soon as you have come

That Blame is just as dear as Praise
And Praise as mere as Blame –

Emily Dickinson (1830–1886)

This is the house that Jack built

This is the house that Jack built.

This is the malt
That lay in the house that Jack built.

This is the rat,
That ate the malt,
That lay in the house that Jack built.

This is the cat,
That kill'd the rat,
That ate the malt,
That lay in the house that Jack built.

This is the dog,
That worried the cat,
That kill'd the rat,
That ate the malt,
That lay in the house that Jack built.

This is the cow with the crumpled horn,
That toss'd the dog,
That worried the cat,
That kill'd the rat,
That ate the malt,
That lay in the house that Jack built.

This is the maiden, all forlorn,
That milk'd the cow with the crumpled horn,
That toss'd the dog,
That worried the cat,
That kill'd the rat,
That ate the malt,
That lay in the house that Jack built.

This is the man all tatter'd and torn,
That kiss'd the maiden all forlorn,
That milk'd the cow with the crumpled horn,
That toss'd the dog,
That worried the cat,
That kill'd the rat,
That ate the malt,
That lay in the house that Jack built.

This is the priest all shaven and shorn,
That married the man all tatter'd and torn,
That kiss'd the maiden all forlorn,
That milk'd the cow with the crumpled horn,
That toss'd the dog,
That worried the cat,
That kill'd the rat,
That ate the malt,
That lay in the house that Jack built.

This is the cock that crow'd in the morn,
That waked the priest all shaven and shorn,
That married the man all tatter'd and torn,
That kiss'd the maiden all forlorn,
That milk'd the cow with the crumpled horn,
That toss'd the dog,
That worried the cat,
That kill'd the rat,
That ate the malt,
That lay in the house that Jack built.

This is the farmer sowing his corn,
That kept the cock that crow'd in the morn,
That waked the priest all shaven and shorn,
That married the man all tatter'd and torn,
That kiss'd the maiden all forlorn,
That milk'd the cow with the crumpled horn,
That toss'd the dog,
That worried the cat,
That kill'd the rat,
That ate the malt,
That lay in the house that Jack built.

Anon.

Crack-a-Dawn

Good day and good morning!
Here is your early morning tea
and here are your crack-a-dawn cereals.
Sugar is also provided.
Breakfast in bed, room service calling!
Are you awake?

Darren, sit up! I'm giving you
ten seconds, starting now! TEN.
The weather outside is fine – at least
by North Sea standards. NINE.
Just a fresh Force Six blowing and a spot
of rain lashing the rooftops. EIGHT.
The sun is shining – lucky Australians!
The bus, however, is on time
according to local radio – SEVEN –
and if you want to walk again and be
reported to the Head that is your business
but – SIX – I have a bus to catch too
and you can pay for a taxi out of your
    pocket money
if I miss it the third morning running.
FIVE. Your gerbil has been eaten by the dog
and the dog has been eaten by a crocodile
that got in down the chimney and is, at
    this moment,
opening its jaws over your toes –
feel it? No? Oh well.

FOUR. A letter has just arrived,
postmarked Wembley, inviting you to play
for England next Saturday against Czechoslovakia –
bet you won't be late for that. THREE.
Czechoslovakia was one of the eighteen spellings
wrong in your Geography homework.
Why wasn't it handed in last week? I found
the letter you forged from your dad
stating you had a dental appointment
on Friday afternoon – TWO – you could
at least have spelt his Christian name right
and the address. Make an appointment with him
an hour after you intend to go out tonight.

ONE. This is your mother speaking
and I am about to pour your tea
over your head, even if it causes me
extra washing. I won't begrudge the powder.
Darren, I'm giving you HALF A SECOND,
  A QUARTER,
AN EIGHTH. No this is not a nightmare,
no the trickle of water you feel at this moment,
is NOT an illusion …

Brian Morse (1948–)

Adam and Eve leave Paradise

(extract from Paradise Lost *Book 12, 1.641)*

In either hand the hastening angel caught
Our lingering parents, and to the Eastern gate
Led them direct, and down the cliff as fast
To the subjected plain – then disappeared.

They, looking back, all the eastern side beheld
Of Paradise, so late their happy seat,
Waved over by that flaming brand, the gate
With dreadful faces thronged and fiery arms.

Some natural tears they dropped, but
   wiped them soon;
      The world was all before them, where
         to choose
      Their place of rest, and Providence
   their guide.
   They, hand in hand, with wandering
steps and slow,
Through Eden took their solitary way.

John Milton (1608–1674)

The Key of the Kingdom

This is the Key of the Kingdom:
In that Kingdom there is a city;
In that city is a town;
In that town there is a street;
In that street there winds a lane;
In that lane there is a yard;
In that yard there is a house;
In that house there waits a room;
In that room an empty bed;
And on that bed a basket –
A basket of sweet flowers
    Of flowers, of flowers;
    A basket of sweet flowers.

Flowers in a basket;
Basket on the bed;
Bed in the chamber;
Chamber in the house;
House in the weedy yard;
Yard in the winding lane;
Lane in the broad street;
Street in the high town;
Town in the city;
City in the Kingdom –
This is the Key of the Kingdom.
  Of the Kingdom this is the Key.

Anon.

poem for ntombe iayo (at five weeks of age)

who them people think
they are putting
me down here
on this floor

i'll just lay
here stretching
my arms and maybe i'll kick
my legs a li'l bit

why i betcha i'll just get up
from here and walk
soons i get big

Nikki Giovanni (1943–)

First Day at School

A millionbillionwillion miles from home
Waiting for the bell to go. (To go where?)
Why are they all so big, other children?
So noisy? So much at home they
must have been born in uniform.
Lived all their lives in playgrounds.
Spent the years inventing games
that don't let me in. Games
that are rough, that swallow you up.

And the railings.
All around, the railings.
Are they to keep out wolves and monsters?
Things that carry off and eat children?
Things you don't take sweets from?
Perhaps they're to stop us getting out.
Running away from the lessins. Lessin.
What does a lessin look like?
Sounds small and slimy.
They keep them in glassrooms.
Whole rooms made out of glass. Imagine.

I wish I could remember my name.
Mummy said it would come in useful.
Like wellies. When there's puddles.
Yellowwellies. I wish she was here.
I think my name is sewn on somewhere.
The teacher will read it for me.
Tea-cher. The one who makes the tea.

Roger McGough (1937–)

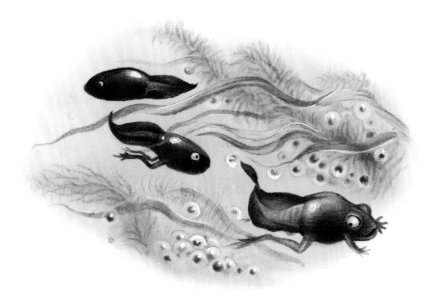

The Tadpole

Underneath the water-weeds
Small and black, I wriggle,
And life is most surprising!
Wiggle! waggle! wiggle!
There's every now and then a most
Exciting change in me,
I wonder, wiggle! waggle!
What I *shall* turn out to be!

Elizabeth Gould (1904–)

A Slash of Blue

A slash of Blue –
A sweep of Gray –
Some scarlet patches on the way,
Compose an Evening Sky –
A little purple – slipped between
Some Ruby Trousers hurried on –
A Wave of Gold –
A Bank of Day –
This just makes out the Morning Sky.

Emily Dickinson (1830–1886)

Mushrooms

Overnight, very
Whitely, discreetly,
Very quietly

Our toes, our noses
Take hold on the loam,
Acquire the air.

Nobody sees us,
Stops us, betrays us;
The small grains make room.

Soft fists insist on
Heaving the needles,
The leafy bedding,

Even the paving.
Our hammers, our rams,
Earless and eyeless.

Perfectly voiceless,
Widen the crannies,
Shoulder through holes. We

Diet on water,
On crumbs of shadow,
Bland-mannered, asking

Little or nothing.
So many of us!
So many of us!

We are shelves, we are
Tables, we are meek,
We are edible,

Nudgers and shovers
In spite of ourselves.
Our kind multiplies:

We shall by morning
Inherit the earth.
Our foot's in the door.

Sylvia Plath (1932–1963)

The Months

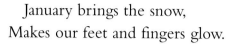

January brings the snow,
Makes our feet and fingers glow.

February brings the rain,
Thaws the frozen lake again.

March brings breezes loud and shrill,
Stirs the dancing daffodil.

April brings the primrose sweet,
Scatters daisies at our feet.

May brings flocks of pretty lambs,
Skipping by their fleecy dams.

June brings tulips, lilies, roses,
Fills the children's hands with posies.

Hot July brings cooling showers,
Apricots and gillyflowers.

August brings the sheaves of corn,
Then the harvest home is borne.

Warm September brings the fruit,
Sportsmen then begin to shoot.

Fresh October brings the pheasant,
Then to gather nuts is pleasant.

Dull November brings the blast,
Then the leaves are whirling fast.

Chill December brings the sleet,
Blazing fire, and Christmas treat.

Sara Coleridge (1802–1852)

Thumbprint

On the pad of my thumb
are whorls, whirls, wheels
in a unique design:
mine alone.
What a treasure to own!
My own flesh, my own feelings.
No other, however grand or base,
can ever contain the same.
My signature,
thumbing the pages of my time.
My universe key,
my singularity.
Impress, implant,
I am myself,
of all my atom parts I am the sum.
And out of my blood and my brain
I make my own interior weather,
my own sun and rain.
Imprint my mark upon the world
whatever I shall become.

Eve Merriam (1916–1992)

Measles in the Ark

The night it was horribly dark,
The measles broke out in the Ark;
Little Japheth, and Shem, and all the young Hams,
Were screaming at once for potatoes and clams.
And 'What shall I do,' said poor Mrs Noah,
'All alone by myself in this terrible shower?
I know what I'll do: I'll step down in the hold,
And wake up a lioness grim and old,
And tie her close to the children's door,
And give her a ginger-cake to roar
At the top of her voice for an hour or more;
And I'll tell the children to cease their din,
Or I'll let that grim old party in,
To stop their squeazles and likewise their
   measles.'
She practised this with the greatest success:
She was everyone's grandmother, I guess.

Susan Coolidge (1835–1905)

The Ark

Nobody knows just how they went.
They certainly went in two by two,
But who preceded the kangaroo
And who dared follow the elephant?

'I've had enough,' said Mrs Noah.
'The food just won't go round,' she said.
A delicate deer raised up his head
As if to say, '*I* want no more.'

In they marched and some were sick.
All very well for those who could be
On the rough or the calm or the middle sea.
But I must say that ark felt very thick

Of food and breath. How wonderful
When the dove appeared and rested upon
The hand of Noah. All fear was gone,
The sea withdrew, the air was cool.

Elizabeth Jennings (1926–)

The Late Passenger

The sky was low, the sounding rain was falling dense
and dark,
And Noah's sons were standing at the window of
the Ark.

The beasts were in, but Japhet said, 'I see one
creature more
Belated and unmated there come knocking at the
door.'

'Well let him knock,' said Ham, 'Or let him drown
or learn to swim.
We're overcrowded as it is; we've got no room for
him.'

'And yet it knocks, how terribly it knocks,' said
Shem, 'Its feet
Are hard as horn – but oh the air that comes from
it is sweet.'

'Now hush,' said Ham, 'You'll waken Dad, and
once he comes to see
What's at the door, it's sure to mean more work for
you and me.'

Noah's voice came roaring from the darkness
    down below,
'Some animal is knocking. Take it in before
    we go.'

Ham shouted back, and savagely he nudged
    the other two,
'That's only Japhet knocking down a brad-nail
    in his shoe.'

Said Noah, 'Boys, I hear a noise that's like a
    horse's hoof.'
Said Ham, 'Why, that's the dreadful rain that drums
    upon the roof.'

Noah tumbled up on deck and out he put
    his head;
His face went grey, His knees were loosed, he tore
    his beard and said,

'Look, look! It would not wait. It turns away. It takes
    its flight.
Fine work you've made of it, my sons, between you
    all tonight!

'Even if I could outrun it now, it would not
    turn again
– Not now. Our great discourtesy has earned its
    high disdain.

'Oh noble and unmated beast, my sons were
    all unkind;
In such a night what stable and what manger will
    you find?

'Oh golden hoofs, oh cataracts of mane,
   oh nostrils wide
With indignation! Oh the neck wave-arched,
   the lovely pride!

'Oh long shall be the furrows ploughed across
   the hearts of men
Before it comes to stable and to manger
   once again,

'And dark and crooked all the ways in which our
   race shall walk,
And shrivelled all their manhood like a flower with
   broken stalk,

'And all the world, oh Ham, may curse the hour
   when you were born
Because of you the Ark must sail without the
   Unicorn.'

C. S. Lewis (1898–1963)

Monday's Child

Monday's child is fair of face,
Tuesday's child is full of grace,
Wednesday's child is full of woe,
Thursday's child has far to go,
Friday's child is loving and giving,
Saturday's child works hard for a living,
But the child that is born on the Sabbath day
Is bonny, and blithe, and good, and gay.

Anon.

The Song of the Sky Loom

O our Mother the Earth, O our Father the Sky,
. . . weave for us a garment of brightness;
May the warp be the white light of morning,
May the weft be the red light of evening,
May the fringes be the falling rain,
May the border be the standing rainbow.
Thus weave for us a garment of brightness
That we may walk fittingly where birds sing,
That we may walk fittingly where grass is green,
O our Mother the Earth, O our father the Sky!

Anon. (Native American)

New Sights

I like to see a thing I know
Has not been seen before,
That's why I cut my apple through
To look into the core.

It's nice to think, though many an eye
Has seen the ruddy skin,
Mine is the very first to spy
The five brown pips within.

Anon.

Salute to the Whole World

You, whoever you are!
You, daughter or son of England!
You of the mighty Slavic tribes and empires!
   You Russ in Russia!
You dim-descended, black, divine-souled African,
   large, fine-headed,
      Nobly-formed, superbly destined, on equal terms
      with me!
You Norwegian, Swede, Dane, Icelander!
   You Prussian!
You Spaniard of Spain, you Portuguese!
You Frenchwoman and Frenchman of France!
You Belge! You liberty-lover of the Netherlands!

You sturdy Austrian! You Lombard, Hun, Bohemian!
　　Farmer of Styria!
You neighbour of the Danube!
You working-man of the Rhine, the Elbe,
　　or the Weser!
　　You working-woman too!
You Sardinian! You Bavarian, Swabian, Saxon,
　　Wallachian, Bulgarian!
You citizen of Prague! Roman, Neapolitan, Greek!
You lithe matador in the arena at Seville!
You mountaineer living lawlessly on the Taurus or
　　Caucasus!
You Bokh horse-herd, watching your mares and
　　stallions feeding!
You beautiful-bodied Persian, at full speed in the
　　saddle, shooting arrows to the mark!
You Chinaman and Chinawoman of China!
　　You Tartar of Tartary!
You women of the earth subordinated at
　　your tasks!
You Jew journeying in your old age through every risk,
　　To stand once more on Syrian ground!
You other Jews waiting in all lands for your Messiah!
You thoughtful Armenian, pondering by some stream
　　of the Euphrates!
You peering amid the ruins of Nineveh!
　　You ascending Mount Ararat!
You foot-worn pilgrim welcoming the far-away
　　sparkle of the minarets of Mecca!

You sheiks along the stretch from Suez to
　　Bab-el-mandeb, ruling your families and tribes!

You olive-grower tending your fruit on fields
of Nazareth, Damascus, or Lake Tiberias!
You Thibet trader on the wide inland, or
bargaining in the shops of Lassa!
You Japanese man or woman! you liver in Madagascar,
Ceylon, Sumatra, Borneo!
All you continentals of Asia, Africa, Europe, Australia,
indifferent of place!
All you on the numberless islands of the
archipelagoes of the sea!
And you of centuries hence, when you listen to me!
And you, each and everywhere, whom I specify not,
but include just the same!
Health to you!
Good will to you all – from me and America sent.
Each of us inevitable;
Each of us limitless – each of us with his or her right
upon the earth;
Each of us allowed the eternal purports of the earth;
Each of us here as divinely as any is here.

Walt Whitman (1819–1892)

WILD & FREE

*'Sharing the sunlight
with the free'*

Leonardo

Leonardo, painter, taking
    Morning air
        On Market Street
Saw the wild birds in their cages
    Silent in
        The dust, the heat.

Took his purse from out his pocket
    Never questioning
        The fee,
Bore the cages to the green shade
    Of a hill-top
        Cypress tree.

'What you lost,' said Leonardo,
    'I now give to you
        Again,
Free as noon and night and morning,
    As the sunshine,
        As the rain.'

And he took them from their prisons,
    Held them to
        The air, the sky;
Pointed them to the bright heaven.
    'Fly!' said Leonardo.
        'Fly!'

Charles Causley (1917–)

Python

Swaggering prince
giant among snakes.
They say python has no house.
I heard it a long time ago
and I laughed and laughed and laughed.
For who owns the ground under the lemon grass?
Who owns the ground under the elephant grass?
Who owns the swamp – father of rivers?
Who owns the stagnant pool – father of waters?

Because they never walk hand in hand
people say that snakes only walk singly.
But just imagine
suppose the viper walks in front
the green mamba follows
and the python creeps rumbling behind –
who will be brave enough
to wait for them?

Anon. (Nigeria)

Wild Bees

These children of the sun which summer brings
As pastoral minstrels in her merry train
Pipe rustic ballads upon busy wings
And glad the cotter's quiet toils again
The white-nosed bee that bores its little hole
In mortared walls and pipes its symphonies
And never-absent couzin black as cole
That Indian-like bepaints its little thighs
With white and red bedight for holiday
Right earlily a morn do pipe and play
And with their legs stroke slumber from their eyes
And aye so fond they of their singing seem
That in their holes abed at close of day
They still keep piping in their honey dreams
And larger ones that thrum on ruder pipe
Round the sweet-smelling closen and rich woods
Where tawney white and red-flushed clover buds
Shine bonnily and beanfields blossom ripe
Shed dainty perfumes and give honey food
To these sweet poets of the summer field
Me much delighting as I stroll along
The narrow path that hay-laid meadow yields
Catching the windings of their wandering song
The black and yellow bumble first on wing
To buzz among the sallow's early flowers
Hiding its nest in holes from fickle spring
Who stints his rambles with her frequent showers
And one that may for wise piper pass
In livery dress half sables and half red
Who laps a moss ball in the meadow grass
And hurds her stores when April showers have fled

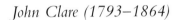

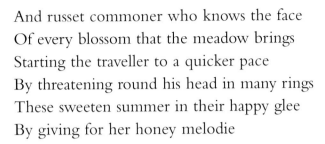

And russet commoner who knows the face
Of every blossom that the meadow brings
Starting the traveller to a quicker pace
By threatening round his head in many rings
These sweeten summer in their happy glee
By giving for her honey melodie

John Clare (1793–1864)

Mary Had a Crocodile

Mary had a crocodile
That ate a child each day;
But interfering people came
And took her pet away.

Anon.

Humming-Bird

I can imagine, in some otherworld
Primeval-dumb, far back
In that most awful stillness, that only gasped and hummed,
Humming-birds raced down the avenues.

Before anything had a soul,
While life was a heave of Matter, half inanimate,
This little bit chipped off in brilliance
And went whizzing through the slow, vast, succulent stems.

I believe there were no flowers, then,
In the world where the humming-bird flashed ahead of
    creation.
I believe he pierced the slow vegetable veins with his
    long beak.

Probably he was big
As mosses, and little lizards, they say were once big.
Probably he was a jabbing, terrifying monster.
We look at him through the wrong end of the long
    telescope of Time,
Luckily for us.

D. H. Lawrence (1885–1930)

'We are going to see the rabbit'

We are going to see the rabbit,
We are going to see the rabbit,
Which rabbit, people say?
Which rabbit, ask the children?
Which rabbit?
The only rabbit,
The only rabbit in England,
Sitting behind a barbed-wire fence
Under the floodlights, neon lights,
Sodium lights,
Nibbling grass
On the only patch of grass
In England, in England
(Except the grass by the hoardings
Which doesn't count.)
We are going to see the rabbit,
And we must be there on time.

First we shall go by escalator,
Then we shall go by underground,
And then we shall go by motorway
And then by helicopterway,
And the last ten yards we shall have to go
On foot.

And now we are going
All the way to see the rabbit.
We are nearly there,
We are longing to see it,
And so is the crowd
Which is here in thousands
With mounted policemen

And big loudspeakers
And bands and banners,
And everyone has come a long way.
But soon we shall see it
Sitting and nibbling
The blades of grass
On the only patch of grass
In – but something has gone wrong!
Why is everyone so angry,
Why is everyone jostling
And slanging and complaining?

The rabbit has gone,
Yes, the rabbit has gone.
He has actually burrowed down into the earth
And made himself a warren, under the earth.
Despite all these people,
And what shall we do?
What *can* we do?

It is all a pity, you must be disappointed.
Go home and do something else for today,
Go home again, go home for today.
For you cannot hear the rabbit, under the earth.
Remarking rather sadly to himself, by himself,
As he rests in his warren, under the earth:
'It won't be long, they are bound to come,
They are bound to come and find me, even here.'

Alan Brownjohn (1931–)

Moth

Pity my silence pressing at your window
Frail and motionless against the night;
A baffled spectre framed by blackness,
Little moonflake, prisoner of glass.
This is my journey's end, receive me.
Brilliant keeper, rise and let me in.

Then later, when from a drawer perhaps
You take my body, wasted, brittle
As a shred of antique parchment, hold it
Gently up to the light I loved
But which bewildered me, until
I fly away again, a ghostly powder
Blown or shaken from your hand.

John Mole (1941–)

To a Mouse

*(On turning her up in her nest with the Plough,
November, 1785)*

Wee, sleekit, cow'rin', tim'rous beastie,
O what a panic's in thy breastie!
Thou need na start awa sae hasty,
   Wi' bickering brattle!†   †scamper
I wad be laith to rin an' chase thee,
   Wi' murd'ring pattle!†   †ploughstaff

I'm truly sorry man's dominion
Has broken Nature's social union,
An' justifies that ill opinion
   Which makes thee startle
At me, thy poor earth-born companion,
   An' fellow-mortal!

I doubt na, whiles, but thou may thieve;
What then? poor beastie, thou maun live!
   A daimen-icker in a thrave†   †ear of corn
   'S a sma' request:
I'll get a blessin' wi' the lave,†   †rest
   And never miss 't!

Thy wee bit housie, too, in ruin!
Its silly wa's the win's are strewin'!
An' naething, now, to big† a new ane,   †build
   O' foggage† green!   †moss
An' bleak December's winds ensuin',
   Baith snell† an' keen!   †bitter

Thou saw the fields laid bare and waste,
An' weary winter comin' fast,
An' cozie here, beneath the blast,
   Thou thought to dwell,
Till crash! the cruel coulter[†] past   [†]ploughshare
   Out-thro' thy cell.

That wee bit heap o' leaves an' stibble[†]   [†]stubble
Hast cost thee mony a weary nibble!
Now thou's turned out, for a' thy trouble,
   But house or hald[†],   [†]homeless
To thole[†] the winter's sleety dribble,   [†]endure
   An' cranreuch[†] cauld!   [†]frost

But, Mousie, thou art no thy lane,[†]   [†]alone
In proving foresight may be vain:
The best laid schemes o' mice an' men
   Gang aft a-gley,[†]   [†]go often astray
An' lea'e us nought but grief an' pain
   For promised joy.

Still thou are blest, compared wi' me!
The present only toucheth thee:
But oh! I backward cast my e'e
   On prospects drear!
An' forward tho' I canna see,
   I guess an' fear!

Robert Burns
(1759–1796)

Lizzy's Lion

Lizzy had a lion
With a big, bad roar,
And she kept him in the bedroom
By the closet-cupboard door;

Lizzy's lion wasn't friendly,
Lizzy's lion wasn't tame –
Not unless you learned to call him
By his Secret Lion Name.

One dark night, a rotten robber
With a rotten robber mask
Snuck in through the bedroom window –
And he didn't even ask.

And he brought a bag of candy
That was sticky-icky-sweet,
Just to make friends with a lion
(If a lion he should meet).

First he sprinkled candy forwards,
Then he sprinkled candy back;
Then he picked up Lizzy's piggy-bank
And stuck it in his sack.

But as the rotten robber
Was preparing to depart,
Good old Lizzy's lion wakened
With a snuffle and a start.

And he muttered, 'Candy? – piffle!'
And he rumbled, 'Candy? – pooh!'
And he gave the rotten robber
An experimental chew.

Then the robber shooed the lion,
Using every name he knew;
But each time he shooed, the lion
Merely took another chew.

It was: 'Down, Fido! Leave, Leo!
Shoo, you good old boy!'
But the lion went on munching
With a look of simple joy.

It was: 'Stop, Mopsy! Scram, Sambo!
This is a disgrace!'
But the lion went on lunching
With a smile upon his face.

Then old Lizzy heard the rumble,
And old Lizzy heard the fight,
And old Lizzy got her slippers
And turned on the bedroom light.

There was robber on the toy-shelf!
There was robber on the rug!
There was robber in the lion
(Who was looking rather smug)!

But old Lizzy wasn't angry,
And old Lizzy wasn't rough.
She simply said the Secret Name:
'*Lion*! – that's enough.'

Then old Lizzy and her Lion
Took the toes & tum & head,
And they put them in the garbage,
And they both went back to bed.

Dennis Lee (1939–)

Never Get Out!

I knew a little Serval cat –
   Never get out!
Would pad all day from this to that –
   Never get out!
From bar to bar she'd turn and turn,
And in her eyes a fire would burn –
(From her Zoology we learn!)
   Never get out!

And if by hap a ray of sun –
Came shining in her cage, she'd run
And sit upon her haunches where
In the open she would stare,
And with the free that sunlight share –
   Never get out!

That catling's jungle heart forlorn
Will die as wild as it was born.
If I could cage the human race
Awhile, like her, in prisoned space,
And teach them what it is to face
   Never get out! . . .

     John Galsworthy (1867–1933)

Anne and the Field-Mouse

We found a mouse in the chalk quarry today
In a circle of stones and empty oil drums
By the fag ends of a fire. There had been
A picnic there; he must have been after the crumbs.

Jane saw him first, a flicker of brown fur
In and out of the charred wood and chalk-white.
I saw him last, but not till we'd turned up
Every stone and surprised him into flight,

Though not far – little zigzag spurts from stone
To stone. Once, as he lurked in his hiding-place,
I saw his beady eyes uplifted to mine.
I'd never seen such terror in so small a face.

I watched, amazed and guilty. Beside us suddenly
A heavy pheasant whirred up from the ground,
Scaring us all; and, before we knew it, the mouse
Had broken cover, skimming away without a sound,

Melting into the nettles. We didn't go
Till I'd chalked in capitals on a rusty can:
THERE'S A MOUSE IN THOSE NETTLES. LEAVE
HIM ALONE. NOVEMBER 15th. ANNE.

Ian Serraillier (1912–1994)

Auguries of Innocence (extract)

To see a World in a grain of sand,
And a Heaven in a wild flower,
Hold Infinity in the palm of your hand,
And Eternity in an hour.

A robin redbreast in a cage
Puts all Heaven in a rage.
A dove-house filled with doves and pigeons
Shudders Hell thro' all its regions.

A dog starved at his master's gate
Predicts the ruin of the State.
A horse misused upon the road
Calls to Heaven for human blood.

Each outcry of the hunted hare
A fibre from the brain does tear.
A skylark wounded in the wing,
A cherubim does cease to sing.

William Blake (1757–1827)

The Eagle

He clasps the crag with crookèd hands;
Close to the sun in lonely lands,
Ring'd with the azure world, he stands.

The wrinkled sea beneath him crawls;
He watches from his mountain walls,
And like a thunderbolt he falls.

Alfred, Lord Tennyson
(1809–1892)

The North Wind Doth Blow

The north wind doth blow,
And we shall have snow,
And what will the robin do then, poor thing?
    He'll sit in a barn,
    And keep himself warm,
And hide his head under his wing, poor thing!

The north wind doth blow,
And we shall have snow,
And what will the swallow do then, poor thing?
  Oh, do you not know
  That he's off long ago,
To a country where he will find spring, poor thing!

The north wind doth blow,
And we shall have snow,
And what will the dormouse do then, poor thing?
  Roll'd up like a ball,
  In his nest snug and small,
He'll sleep till warm weather comes in, poor thing!

The north wind doth blow,
And we shall have snow,
And what will the honey-bee do then, poor thing?
  In his hive he will stay
  Till the cold is away,
And then he'll come out in the spring, poor thing!

The north wind doth blow,
And we shall have snow,
And what will the children do then, poor things?
  When lessons are done,
  They must skip, jump and run,
Until they have made themselves warm, poor things!

Anon.

The Dromedary

In dreams I see the Dromedary still,
   As once in a gay park I saw him stand.
   A thousand eyes in vulgar wonder scanned
His hump and hairy neck, and gazed their fill
At his lank shanks and mocked with laughter shrill.
   He never moved: and if his Eastern land
   Flashed on his eye with stretches of hot sand,
It wrung no mute appeal from his proud will.

He blinked upon the rabble lazily;
   And still some trace of majesty forlorn
And a coarse grace remained: his head was high,
   Though his gaunt flanks with a great mange were worn;
There was not any yearning in his eye,
   But on his lips and nostril infinite scorn.

A.Y. Campbell (1925–)

The Fallow Deer at the Lonely House

One without looks in tonight
   Through the curtain-chink
From the sheet of glistening white;
One without looks in tonight
   As we sit and think
   By the fender-brink.

We do not discern those eyes
   Watching in the snow;
Lit by lamps of rosy dyes
We do not discern those eyes
   Wondering, aglow,
   Fourfooted, tiptoe.

Thomas Hardy (1840–1928)

Lullaby for a Baby Toad

Sleep, my child:
The dark dock leaf
Spreads a tent
To hide your grief.
The thing you saw
In the forest pool
When you bent to drink
In the evening cool
Was a mask that He,
The Wisest Toad,
Gave us to hide
Our precious load –
The jewel that shines
In the flat toad-head,
With gracious sapphire
And changing red.

For if, my toadling,
Your face were fair
As the precious jewel
That glimmers there,
Man, the jealous,
Man, the cruel,
Would look at you
And suspect the jewel.

So dry the tears
From your hornèd eyes,
And eat your supper
Of dew and flies;
Curl in the shade
Of the nettles deep,
Think of your jewel
And go to sleep.

Stella Gibbons (1902–)

The Two Roots

A pair of pine roots, old and dark,
make conversation in the park.

The whispers where the top leaves grow
are echoed in the roots below.

An agèd squirrel sitting there
is knitting stockings for the pair.

The one says: squeak. The other: squawk.
That is enough for one day's talk.

Christian Morgenstern (1817–1914)
translated from the German

How Doth the Little Crocodile

How doth the little crocodile
Improve his shining tail;
And pour the waters of the Nile
On every golden scale!

How cheerfully he seems to grin,
How neatly spreads his claws,
And welcomes little fishes in,
With gently smiling jaws!

Lewis Carroll (1832–1898)

I Saw a Jolly Hunter

I saw a jolly hunter
With a jolly gun
Walking in the country
In the jolly sun.

In the jolly meadow
Sat a jolly hare.
Saw the jolly hunter.
Took jolly care.

Hunter jolly eager –
Sight of jolly prey.
Forgot gun pointing
Wrong jolly way.

Jolly hunter jolly head
Over heels gone.
Jolly old safety-catch
Not jolly on.

Bang went the jolly gun.
Hunter jolly dead.
Jolly hare got clean away.
Jolly good, I said.

Charles Causley (1917–)

Little Trotty Wagtail

Little trotty wagtail, he went in the rain,
And tittering, tottering sideways he ne'er got straight again,
He stooped to get a worm, and looked up to catch a fly,
And then he flew away ere his feathers they were dry.

Little trotty wagtail, he waddled in the mud,
And left his little footmarks, trample where he would.
He waddled in the water-pudge, and waggle went his tail,
And chirrupt up his wings to dry upon the garden rail.

Little trotty wagtail, you nimble all about,
And in the dimpling water-pudge you waddle in and out;
Your home is nigh at hand, and in the warm pigsty,
So, little Master Wagtail, I'll bid you a good-bye.

John Clare (1793–1864)

Whale

A whale lay cast up on the island's shore
   in the shallow water of the outgoing tide.
     He struggled to fill his lungs,
    he grew acquainted with weight.

And the people came and said, Kill it, it is food.
And the witch-doctor said, It is sacred, it must not be harmed.
And a girl came and with an empty coconut-shell
   scooped the seawater and let it run over the whale's blue bulk.

A small desperate eye showing white all round
   the dark iris. The great head flattened against
     sand as a face pressed against glass.

And a white man came and said, If all the people
   push we can float it off on the next tide.
And the witch-doctor said, It is taboo, it must not be touched.

And the people drifted away.
And the white man cursed and ran off to the next village for help.

And the girl stayed.
She stayed as the tide went out.
The whale's breath came in harsh spasms.
Its skin was darkening in the sun.
The girl got children to form a chain
of coconut-shells filled with fresh water
that she poured over his skin.

The whale's eye seemed calmer.

With the high tide the white man came back.
As the whale felt sea reach to his eye he reared
on fins and tail flukes, his spine arced
and he slapped it all down together, a great leap
into the same inert sand.

His eye rolled
in panic as again he lifted and crashed down,
   exhausted, and again lifted and crashed down,
      and again, and again.

The white man couldn't bear his agony and strode away,
   as the tide receded.
He paced and paced the island and cursed God.

Now the whale didn't move.
The girl stroked his head
and as the moon came up
she sang to him
of friends long dead and children grown and gone,
sang like a mother to the whale,

and sang of unrequited love.

And later in the night
   when his breaths had almost lost touch
      she leant her shoulder against his cheek

and told him stories, with many details,
of the mud-skipping fish that lived
      in the mangroves on the lagoon.

Her voice
and its coaxing pauses
was as if fins
were bearing him up to the surface of the ocean
to breathe and see,
as with a clot of blood falling on her brow
the whale passed clear from the body of his death.

                              D. M. Thomas (1914–1953)

PETS & FRIENDS

*'You own the freedom
we have lost'*

The Riding School

We are at grass now and the emerald meadow
Highlights our polished coats. All afternoon
You trotted, cantered us. How mild we were,
Our bodies were at one
With yours. Now we are cropping at the shadow
We throw. We scarcely stir.

You never saw us wild or being broken
In. We tossed our saddles off and ran
With streaming manes. Like Pegasus almost
We scorned the air. A man
Took long to tame us. Let your words be spoken
Gently. You own the freedom we have lost.

Elizabeth Jennings (1926–)

I Had a Little Pony

I had a little pony,
His name was Dapple-grey.
I lent him to a lady,
To ride a mile away.

She whipped him, she lashed him,
She drove him through the mire,
I wouldn't lend my pony now,
For all the lady's hire.

Anon.

The Prayer of the Foal

O God! The grass is so young
My hooves are full of capers.
Then
why does this terror start up in me?
I race
and my mane catches the wind.
I race
and Your scents beat on my heart.
I race,
falling over my own feet in my joy.
because my eyes are too big
and I am their prisoner:
eyes too quick to seize
on the uneasiness that runs through the
    whole world.
Dear God,
when the strange night
prowls round the edge of day,
let Yourself be moved by my plaintive whinny;
set a star to watch over me
and hush my fear.

Amen

Carmen Bernos de Gasztold (d. 1996)
translated from the French
by Rumer Godden (1907–)

To a Black Greyhound

Shining black in the shining light,
  Inky black in the golden sun,
Graceful as the swallow's flight,
  Light as swallow, wingèd one,
Swift as driven hurricane –
  Double-sinewed stretch and spring,
Muffled thud of flying feet,
  See the black dog galloping,
  Hear his wild foot-beat.

See him lie when the day is dead,
  Black curves curled on the boarded floor.
Sleepy eyes, my sleepy-head –
  Eyes that were aflame before.
Gentle now, they burn no more;
  Gentle now and softly warm,
With the fire that made them bright
  Hidden – as when after storm
  Softly falls the night.

God of speed, who makes the fire –
  God of Peace, who lulls the same –
God who gives the fierce desire,
  Lust for blood as fierce as flame –
God who stands in Pity's name –
  Many may ye be or less,
Ye who rule the earth and sun:
  Gods of strength and gentleness,
  Ye are ever one.

Julian Grenfell (1888–1915)

Lone Dog

I'm a lean dog, a keen dog, a wild dog, and lone;
I'm a rough dog, a tough dog, hunting on my own;
I'm a bad dog, a mad dog, teasing silly sheep;
I love to sit and bay the moon, to keep fat souls from sleep.

I'll never be a lap dog, licking dirty feet,
A sleek dog, a meek dog, cringing for my meat;
Not for me the fireside, the well-filled plate,
But shut door, and sharp stone, and cuff, and kick, and hate.

Not for me the other dogs, running by my side;
Some have run a short while, but none of them would bide,
O mine is still the lone trail, the hard trail, the best,
Wide wind, and wild stars, and the hunger of the quest!

Irene McLeod (1891–?)

The Donkey

When fishes flew and forests walked
And figs grew upon thorn,
Some moment when the moon was blood
Then surely I was born;

With monstrous head and sickening cry
And ears like errant wings,
The devil's walking parody
Of all four-footed things.

The tattered outlaw of the earth,
Of ancient crooked will;
Starve, scourge, deride me: I am dumb,
I keep my secret still.

Fools! For I also had my hour;
One far fierce hour and sweet:
There was a shout about my ears,
And palms before my feet.

G. K. Chesterton (1874–1936)

Poor Dog Tray

On the green banks of Shannon when Sheelah was nigh,
No blithe Irish lad was so happy as I;
No harp like my own could so cheerily play,
And wherever I went was my poor dog Tray.

When at last I was forced from my Sheelah to part,
She said (while the sorrow was big at her heart),
Oh! remember your Sheelah when far, far away:
And be kind, my dear Pat, to our poor dog Tray.

Poor dog! he was faithful and kind to be sure,
And he constantly loved me although I was poor;
When the sour-looking folk sent me heartless away,
I had always a friend in my poor dog Tray.

When the road was so dark, and the night was so cold,
And Pat and his dog were grown weary and old,
How snugly we slept in my old coat of grey,
And he lick'd me for kindness – my old dog Tray.

Though my wallet was scant I remember'd his case,
Nor refused my last crust to his pitiful face;
But he died at my feet on a cold winter day,
And I play'd a sad lament for my poor dog Tray.

Where now shall I go, poor, forsaken, and blind?
Can I find one to guide me, so faithful and kind?
To my sweet native village, so far, far away,
I can never more return with my poor dog Tray.

Thomas Campbell (1777–1844)

Duck's Ditty

All along the backwater,
Through the rushes tall,
Ducks are a-dabbling,
Up tails all!

Ducks' tails, drakes' tails,
Yellow feet a-quiver,
Yellow bills all out of sight
Busy in the river!

Slushy green undergrowth
Where the roach swim,
Here we keep our larder
Cool and full and dim!

Every one for what he likes!
We like to be
Heads down, tails up,
Dabbling free!

High in the blue above
Swifts whirl and call –
We are down a-dabbling,
Up tails all!

Kenneth Grahame
(1859–1932)

The Duck

Behold the duck.
It does not cluck.
A cluck it lacks.
It quacks.
It is specially fond
Of a puddle or pond.
When it dines or sups,
It bottoms ups.

Ogden Nash
(1902–1971)

Mary's Lamb

Mary had a little lamb,
Its fleece was white as snow,
And everywhere that Mary went
The lamb was sure to go;
He followed her to school one day –
That was against the rule,
It made the children laugh and play
To see a lamb at school.

And so the teacher turned him out,
But still he lingered near,
And waited patiently about,
Till Mary did appear.
And then he ran to her and laid
His head upon her arm,
As if he said, 'I'm not afraid –
You'll shield me from all harm.'

'What makes the lamb love Mary so?'
The little children cry;
'Oh, Mary loves the lamb, you know,'
The teacher did reply,
'And you each gentle animal
In confidence may bind,
And make it follow at your call,
If you are always kind.'

Sarah Josepha Hale (1788–1879)

The Sheep

Slowly they pass
In the grey of the evening
Over the wet road,
A flock of sheep.
Slowly they wend
In the grey of the gloaming
Over the wet road
That winds through the town.
Slowly they pass,
And gleaming whitely
Vanish away
In the grey of the evening.

Seumas O'Sullivan
(1879–1958)

Cows on the Beach

Two cows,
fed-up with grass, field, farmer,
barged through barbed wire
and found the beach.
Each mooed to each:
This is a better place to be,
a stretch of sand next to the sea,
this is the place for me.
And they stayed there all day,
strayed this way, that way,
over to rocks,
past discarded socks,
ignoring the few people they met
(it wasn't high season yet).
They dipped hooves in the sea,
got wet up to the knee,
they swallowed pebbles and sand,
found them a bit bland,
washed them down with sea-water,
decided they really ought to
rest for an hour.
Both were sure
they'd never leave here.
Imagine, they'd lived so near
and never knew!
With a swapped moo
they sank into sleep,
woke to the yellow jeep
of the farmer
revving there
feet from the incoming sea.

This is no place for cows to be,
he shouted, and slapped them
with seaweed, all the way home.

Matthew Sweeney (1952–)

The Cow

The friendly cow, all red and white,
I love with all my heart:
She gives me cream with all her might,
To eat with apple-tart.

She wanders lowing here and there,
And yet she cannot stray,
All in the pleasant open air,
The pleasant light of day;

And blown by all the winds that pass
And wet with all the showers,
She walks among the meadow grass
And eats the meadow flowers.

R. L. Stevenson (1850–1894)

Cows

Half the time they munched the grass, and all the time they lay
Down in the water-meadows, the lazy month of May,
          A-chewing,
          A-mooing,
     To pass the hours away.

          'Nice weather,' said the brown cow.
               'Ah,' said the white.
          'Grass is very tasty.'
               'Grass is all right.'

Half the time they munched the grass, and all the time they lay
Down in the water-meadows, the lazy month of May,
          A-chewing,
          A-mooing,
     To pass the hours away.

          'Rain coming,' said the brown cow.
               'Ah,' said the white.
          'Flies is very tiresome.'
               'Flies bite.'

Half the time they munched the grass, and all the time they lay
Down in the water-meadows, the lazy month of May,
          A-chewing,
          A-mooing,
     To pass the hours away.

          'Time to go,' said the brown cow.
               'Ah,' said the white.
          'Nice chat.' 'Very pleasant.'
               'Night.' 'Night.'

Half the time they munched the grass, and all the time they lay
Down in the water-meadows, the lazy month of May,
      A-chewing,
      A-mooing,
    To pass the hours away.

James Reeves (1909–1978)

Cats

        Cats sleep
         Anywhere,
          Any table,
           Any chair,
          Top of piano,
         Window-ledge,
         In the middle,
          On the edge,
          Open drawer,
Anybody's
Lap will do,
  Fitted in a
  Cardboard box,
   In the cupboard
    With your frocks –
     Anywhere!
      They don't care!
     Cats sleep
      Anywhere.

          Empty shoe,

Eleanor Farjeon (1881–1965)

The Prayer of the Cat

Lord,
I am the cat,
It is not, exactly, that I have something to ask of You!
No –
I ask nothing of anyone –
but,
if You have by some chance, in some celestial barn,
a little white mouse,
or a saucer of milk,
I know someone who would relish them.
Wouldn't You like some day
to put a curse on the whole race of dogs?
If so I should say,

Amen

Carmen Bernos de Gasztold (d.1996)
translated from the French
by Rumer Godden (1907–)

The Horses

I climbed through woods in the hour-before-dawn dark.
Evil air, a frost-making stillness,

Not a leaf, not a bird, –
A world cast in frost. I came out above the wood

Where my breath left tortuous statues in the iron light.
But the valleys were draining the darkness

Till the moorline – blackening dregs of the brightening grey –
Halved the sky ahead. And I saw the horses:

Huge in the dense grey – ten together –
Megalith-still. They breathed, making no move,

With draped manes and tilted hind-hooves,
Making no sound.

I passed: not one snorted or jerked its head.
Grey silent fragments

Of a grey silent world.

I listened in emptiness on the moor-ridge.
The curlew's tear turned its edge on the silence.

Slowly detail leafed from the darkness. Then the sun
Orange, red, red erupted.

Silently, and splitting to its core tore and flung cloud,
Shook the gulf open, showed blue,

And the big planets hanging –
I turned

Stumbling in the fever of a dream, down towards
The dark woods, from the kindling tops,

And came to the horses.
There, still they stood,
But now steaming and glistening under the flow of light,

Their draped stone manes, their tilted hind-hooves
Stirring under a thaw while all around them

The frost showed its fires. But still they made no sound.
Not one snorted or stamped,

Their hung heads patient as the horizons
High over valleys, in the red levelling rays –

In din of the crowded streets, going among the years, the faces,
May I still meet my memory in so lonely a place

Between the streams and the red clouds, hearing curlews,
Hearing the horizons endure.

Ted Hughes (1930–)

The Cat and the Moon

The cat went here and there
And the moon spun round like a top,
And the nearest kin of the moon,
The creeping cat, looked up.
Black Minnaloushe stared at the moon,
For, wander and wail as he would,
The pure cold light in the sky
Troubled his animal blood.
Minnaloushe runs in the grass
Lifting his delicate feet.
Do you dance, Minnaloushe, do you dance?

When two close kindred meet,
What better than call a dance?
Maybe the moon may learn,
Tired of that courtly fashion,
A new dance turn.
Minnaloushe creeps through the grass
From moonlit place to place,
The sacred moon overhead
Has taken a new phase.
Does Minnaloushe know that his pupils
Will pass from change to change,
And that from round to crescent,
From crescent to round they range?
Minnaloushe creeps through the grass
Alone, important and wise,
And lifts to the changing moon
His changing eyes.

W. B. Yeats
(1865–1939)

The Kitten and the Falling Leaves

See the Kitten on the wall,
Sporting with the leaves that fall,
Withered leaves – one-two-and three –
From the lofty elder-tree!
Through the calm and frosty air
Of this morning bright and fair,
Eddying round and round they sink
Softly, slowly: one might think,
From the motions that are made,
Every little leaf conveyed
Sylph or Faery hither tending,
To this lower world descending,
Each invisible and mute
In his wavering parachute.

– But the Kitten, how she starts,
Crouches, stretches, paws, and darts!
First at one, and then its fellow
Just as light and just as yellow.
There are many now – now one –
Now they stop and there are none:
What intenseness of desire
In her upward eye of fire!
With a tiger-leap half-way
Now she meets the coming prey,
Lets it go as fast, and then
Has it in her power again:
Now she works with three or four,
Like an Indian conjurer;
Quick as he in feats of art,
Far beyond in joy of heart.

Were her antics played in the eye
Of a thousand standers-by,
Clapping hands with shout and stare,
What would little Tabby care
For the plaudits of the crowd?

William Wordsworth (1770–1850)

To a Cat

Stately, kindly, lordly friend.
   Condescend
Here to sit by me, and turn
Glorious eyes that smile and burn,
Golden eyes, love's lustrous meed,
On the golden page I read.

All your wondrous wealth of hair,
   Dark and fair,
Silken-shaggy, soft and bright
As the clouds and beams of night,
Pays my reverent hand's caress
Back with friendlier gentleness.

Dogs may fawn on all and some
   As they come;
You, a friend of loftier mind,
Answer friends alone in kind,
Just your foot upon my hand
Softly bids it understand.

A. C. Swinburne
(1837–1909)

The Donkey

I saw a donkey
One day old,
His head was too big
For his neck to hold;
His legs were shaky
And long and loose,
They rocked and staggered
And weren't much use.

He tried to gambol
And frisk a bit,
But he wasn't quite sure
Of the trick of it.
His queer little coat
Was soft and grey,
And curled at his neck
In a lovely way.
His face was wistful
And left no doubt
That he felt life needed
Some thinking about.
So he blundered round
In venturesome quest,
And then lay flat
On the ground to rest.

He looked so little
And weak and slim,
I prayed the world
Might be good to him.

Anon.

WEIRD & WONDERFUL

'Moonlight, summer moonlight'

Something Told the Wild Geese

Something told the wild geese
It was time to go,
Though the fields lay golden
Something whispered, 'Snow!'
Leaves were green and stirring,
Berries lustre-glossed,
But beneath warm feathers
Something cautioned, 'Frost!'

All the sagging orchards
Steamed with amber spice,
But each wild beast stiffened
At remembered ice.
Something told the wild geese
It was time to fly –
Summer sun was on their wings,
Winter in their cry.

Rachel Field (1894–1942)

Moonlit Apples

At the top of the house the apples are laid in rows,
And the skylight lets the moonlight in, and those
Apples are deep-sea apples of green. There goes
　A cloud on the moon in the autumn night.

A mouse in the wainscot scratches, and scratches, and then
There is no sound at the top of the house of men
Or mice; and the cloud is blown, and the moon again
　Dapples the apples with deep-sea light.

They are lying in rows there, under the gloomy beams;
On the sagging floor; they gather the silver streams
Out of the moon, those moonlit apples of dreams,
　And quiet is the steep stair under.

In the corridors under there is nothing but sleep.
And stiller than ever on orchard boughs they keep
Tryst with the moon, and deep is the silence, deep
　On moon-washed apples of wonder.

John Drinkwater (1882–1937)

Ozymandias

I met a traveller from an antique land
Who said: Two vast and trunkless legs of stone
Stand in the desert. Near them on the sand,
Half sunk, a shatter'd visage lies, whose frown
And wrinkled lip and sneer of cold command
Tell that its sculptor well those passions read
Which yet survive, stamp'd on these lifeless things.
The hand that mock'd them and the heart that fed;
And on the pedestal these words appear:
'My name is Ozymandias, king of kings:
Look on my works, ye Mighty, and despair!'
Nothing beside remains. Round the decay
Of that colossal wreck, boundless and bare,
The lone and level sands stretch far away.

P. B. Shelley (1792–1822)

Overheard on a Saltmarsh

Nymph, nymph, what are your beads?

Green glass, goblin. Why do you stare at them?

Give them me.

No.

Give them me. Give them me.

No.

Then I will howl all night in the reeds,
Lie in the mud and howl for them.

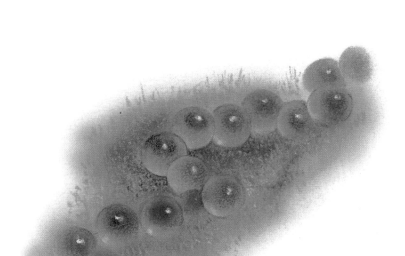

Goblin, why do you love them so?

They are better than stars or water,
Better than voices of winds that sing,
Better than any man's fair daughter,
Your green glass beads on a silver ring.

Hush, I stole them out of the moon.

Give me your beads, I desire them.

No.

I will howl in a deep lagoon
For your green glass beads, I love them so,
Give them me. Give them.

No.

Harold Monro (1879–1932)

The Tyger

Tyger! Tyger! burning bright
In the forests of the night,
What immortal hand or eye
Could frame thy fearful symmetry?

In what distant deeps or skies
Burnt the fire of thine eyes?
On what wings dare he aspire?
What the hand dare seize the fire?

And what shoulder, and what art,
Could twist the sinews of thy heart?
And when thy heart began to beat,
What dread hand? and what dread feet?

What the hammer? what the chain?
In what furnace was thy brain?
What the anvil? what dread grasp
Dare its deadly terrors clasp?

When the stars threw down their spears,
And water'd heaven with their tears,
Did he smile his work to see?
Did he who made the Lamb make thee?

Tyger! Tyger! burning bright
In the forests of the night,
What immortal hand or eye,
Dare frame thy fearful symmetry?

William Blake (1757–1827)

La Belle Dame sans Merci

O what can ail thee, knight-at-arms,
Alone and palely loitering?
The sedge is wither'd from the lake,
And no birds sing.

O what can ail thee, knight-at-arms,
So haggard and so woe-begone?
The squirrel's granary is full,
And the harvest's done.

I see a lily on thy brow
With anguish moist and fever dew;
And on thy cheek a fading rose
Fast withereth too.

'I met a lady in the meads,
Full beautiful – a faery's child,
Her hair was long, her foot was light,
And her eyes were wild.

'I made a garland for her head,
And bracelets too, and fragrant zone;
She look'd at me as she did love,
And made sweet moan.

'I set her on my pacing steed
And nothing else saw all day long,
For sideways would she lean, and sing
A faery's song.

'She found me roots of relish sweet,
And honey wild and manna dew,
And sure in language strange she said,
"I love thee true!"

'She took me to her elfin grot,
And there she wept and sigh'd full sore;
And there I shut her wild, wild eyes
With kisses four.

'And there she lullèd me asleep,
And there I dream'd – Ah! woe betide!
The latest dream I ever dream'd
On the cold hill's side.

'I saw pale kings and princes too,
Pale warriors, death-pale were they all;
Who cried – "La belle Dame sans Merci
Hath thee in thrall!"

'I saw their starved lips in the gloam
With horrid warning gapèd wide,
And I awoke and found me here
On the cold hill's side.

'And this is why I sojourn here
Alone and palely loitering,
Though the sedge is wither'd from the lake,
And no birds sing.'

John Keats (1795–1821)

Full Moon and Little Frieda

A cool small evening shrunk to a dog bark and the
    clank of a bucket –

And you listening.
A spider's web, tense for the dew's touch.
A pail lifted, still and brimming – mirror
To tempt a first star to a tremor.

Cows are going home in the lane there, looping the
    hedges with their warm wreaths of breath –
A dark river of blood, many boulders,
Balancing unspilled milk.

'Moon!' you cry suddenly, 'Moon! Moon!'

The moon has stepped back like an artist gazing
    amazed at a work

That points at him amazed.

Ted Hughes (1930–)

Moonlight, Summer Moonlight

'Tis moonlight, summer moonlight,
All soft and still and fair;
The silent time of midnight
Shines sweetly everywhere,

But most where trees are sending
Their breezy boughs on high,
Or stooping low are lending
A shelter from the sky.

Emily Brontë (1818–1848)

King David

King David was a sorrowful man:
No cause for his sorrow had he;
And he called for the music of a hundred harps,
To ease his melancholy.

They played till they all fell silent:
Played – and play sweet did they;
But the sorrow that haunted the heart of King David
They could not charm away.

He rose; and in his garden
Walked by the moon alone,
A nightingale hidden in a cypress-tree
Jargoned on and on.

King David lifted his sad eyes
Into the dark-boughed tree –
'Tell me, thou little bird that singest,
Who taught my grief to thee?'

But the bird in no wise heeded;
And the king in the cool of the moon
Hearkened to the nightingale's sorrowfulness,
Till all his own was gone.

Walter de la Mare (1873–1956)

Kubla Khan

In Xanadu did Kubla Khan
A stately pleasure-dome decree:
Where Alph, the sacred river, ran
Through caverns measureless to man
　Down to a sunless sea.
So twice five miles of fertile ground
With walls and towers were girdled round:
And here were gardens bright with sinuous rills,
Where blossomed many an incense-bearing tree;
And here were forests ancient as the hills
Enfolding sunny spots of greenery.

But oh! that deep romantic chasm which slanted
Down the green hill athwart a cedarn cover!
A savage place! as holy and enchanted
As e'er beneath a waning moon was haunted
By woman wailing for her demon-lover!
And from this chasm, with ceaseless turmoil seething,
As if this earth in fast thick pants were breathing,
A mighty fountain momently was forced:
Amid whose swift half-intermitted burst
Huge fragments vaulted like rebounding hail,
Or chaffy grain beneath the thresher's flail;
And 'mid these dancing rocks at once and ever
It flung up momently the sacred river.
Five miles meandering with a mazy motion
Through wood and dale the sacred river ran,
Then reached the caverns measureless to man,
And sank in tumult to a lifeless ocean:
And 'mid this tumult Kubla heard from far
Ancestral voices prophesying war!

The shadow of the dome of pleasure
Floated midway on the waves;
Where was heard the mingled measure
From the fountain and the caves.
It was a miracle of rare device,
A sunny pleasure-dome with caves of ice!
A damsel with a dulcimer
In a vision once I saw:
It was an Abyssinian maid,
And on her dulcimer she played,
Singing of Mount Abora.
Could I revive within me
Her symphony and song,
To such a deep delight 'twould win me,
That with music loud and long,
I would build that dome in air,
That sunny dome! those caves of ice!
And all who heard should see them there,
And all should cry, Beware! Beware!
His flashing eyes, his floating hair!
Weave a circle round him thrice,
And close your eyes with holy dread,
For he on honey-dew hath fed,
And drunk the milk of Paradise.

S. T. Coleridge (1772–1834)

The Listeners

'Is there anybody there?' said the Traveller,
Knocking on the moonlit door;
And his horse in the silence champed the grasses
Of the forest's ferny floor;
And a bird flew up out of the turret,
Above the Traveller's head:
And he smote upon the door again a second time;
'Is there anybody there?' he said.
But no one descended to the Traveller;
No head from the leaf-fringed sill
Leaned over and looked into his grey eyes,
Where he stood perplexed and still.
But only a host of phantom listeners
That dwelt in the lone house then
Stood listening in the quiet of the moonlight
To that voice from the world of men:
Stood thronging the faint moonbeams on the dark stair,
That goes down to the empty hall,
Hearkening in an air stirred and shaken
By the lonely Traveller's call.
And he felt in his heart their strangeness,
Their stillness answering his cry,
While his horse moved, cropping the dark turf,
'Neath the starred and leafy sky;
For he suddenly smote on the door, even
Louder, and lifted his head: –
'Tell them I came, and no one answered,
That I kept my word,' he said.

Never the least stir made the listeners,
Though every word he spake
Fell echoing through the shadowiness of the still house
From the one man left awake:
Ay, they heard his foot upon the stirrup,
And the sound of iron on stone,
And how the silence surged softly backward,
When the plunging hoofs were gone.

Walter de la Mare (1873–1956)

The Fairies

Up the airy mountain,
Down the rushy glen,
We daren't go a-hunting
For fear of little men;
Wee folk, good folk,
Trooping all together;
Green jacket, red cap,
And white owl's feather!

Down along the rocky shore
Some make their home,
They live on crispy pancakes
Of yellow tide-foam;
Some in the reeds
Of the black mountain lake,
With frogs for their watch-dogs,
All night awake.

High on the hill-top
The old King sits;
He is now so old and gray
He's nigh lost his wits.
With a bridge of white mist
Columbkill he crosses,
On his stately journeys
From Slieveleague to Rosses;
Or going up with music
On cold starry nights
To sup with the Queen
Of the gay Northern Lights.

They stole little Bridget
For seven years long;
When she came down again
Her friends were all gone.
They took her lightly back,
Between the night and morrow,
They thought that she was fast asleep,
But she was dead with sorrow.
They have kept her ever since
Deep within the lake,
On a bed of flag-leaves,

Watching till she wake.
By the craggy hill-side,
Through the mosses bare,
They have planted thorn-trees
For pleasure here and there.
If any man so daring
As dig them up in spite,
He shall find their sharpest thorns
In his bed at night.

Up the airy mountain,
Down the rushy glen,
We daren't go a-hunting
For fear of little men;
Wee folk, good folk,
Trooping all together;
Green jacket, red cap,
And white owl's feather!

William Allingham
(1824–1889)

The Burmese Cats

I

Once we went out for a walk, in the park, or by the river.
It was a Sunday, or a holiday, I don't quite remember which
    any more.
Anyway, it was good weather, and we both enjoyed our walk
    and the weather.
And, as we walked, we came up from the river past a high wall.

II

And on the wall two beautiful Burmese cats were walking, near
    an open window.
It was one of those lyrical moments you read about, and
    sometimes remember later.
The two cats in withering sunlight, and the two of us looking up.
I suppose you could say it was a kind of awakening, or a vision.

III

Except that the two Burmese cats were just cats, and we were
    just us.
Afterwards, we went on with our walk, across the Green, and
    got home.
I expect we had tea, with perhaps toast and some chocolate or
    ginger cake.
And I would have read a book, or the papers, if it was Sunday.

IV

I don't remember any other details now, you see, except that
    this happened.
The sun shone, we had our walk, and there were two beautiful
    Burmese cats.

George Macbeth (1932–)

Windy Nights

Whenever the moon and stars are set,
  Whenever the wind is high,
All night long in the dark and wet,
  A man goes riding by.
Late in the night when the fires are out,
Why does he gallop and gallop about?

Whenever the trees are crying aloud,
  And ships are tossed at sea,
By, on the highway, low and loud,
  By at the gallop goes he.
By at the gallop he goes, and then
By he comes back at the gallop again.

R. L. Stevenson (1850–1894)

Inversnaid

This darksome burn, horseback brown,
His rollrock highroad roaring down,
In coop† and in comb§ the fleece of his foam   †hollow §crest
Flutes and low to the lake falls home.

A windpuff-bonnet of fáwn-fróth
Turns and twindles over the broth
Of a pool so pitchblack, féll-frówning,
It rounds and rounds Despair to drowning.

Degged with dew, dappled with dew
Are the groins of the braes that the brook treads through,
Wiry heathpacks, flitches of fern,   †heather
And the beadbonny ash that sits over the burn.

What would the world be, once bereft
Of wet and of wildness? Let them be left,
O let them be left, wildness and wet;
Long live the weeds and the wilderness yet.

Gerard Manley Hopkins (1844–1889)

Jabberwocky

'Twas brillig, and the slithy toves
Did gyre and gimble in the wabe:
All mimsy were the borogoves.
And the mome raths outgrabe.

'Beware the Jabberwock, my son!
The jaws that bite, the claws that catch!
Beware the Jubjub bird, and shun
The frumious Bandersnatch!'

He took his vorpal sword in hand:
Long time the manxome foe he sought –
So rested he by the Tumtum tree,
And stood awhile in thought.

And, as in uffish thought he stood,
The Jabberwock, with eyes of flame,
Came whiffling through the tulgey wood,
And burbled as it came!

One, two! One, two! And through and through
The vorpal blade went snicker-snack!
He left it dead, and with its head
He went galumphing back.

'And hast thou slain the Jabberwock?
Come to my arms, my beamish boy!
O frabjous day! Callooh! Callay!'
He chortled in his joy.

'Twas brillig, and the slithy toves
Did gyre and gimble in the wabe:
All mimsy were the borogoves,
And the mome raths outgrabe.

Lewis Carroll (1832–1898)

Lowery Cot

for Robert Graves

This is the house where Jesse White
Run staring in one misty night,
And said he seed the Holy Ghost
Out to Lowery finger-post.

Said It rised up like a cloud
Muttering to Itself out loud,
And stood tremendous on the hill
While all the breathing world was still.

They put en shivering to bed,
And in three days the man was dead.
Gert solemn visions such as they
Be overstrong for mortal clay.

L. A. G. Strong (1896–1958)

HILL & DALE

*'O, wild birds,
come and nest in me!'*

The Babes in the Wood

My dear, do you know
How a long time ago,
    Two poor little children,
Whose names I don't know,
Were stolen away
On a fine summer's day,
    And left in a wood,
As I've heard people say.

And when it was night,
So sad was their plight,
    The sun it went down,
And the moon gave no light!
They sobbed and they sighed,
And they bitterly cried,
    And the poor little things,
They lay down and died.

And when they were dead,
The robins so red
  Brought strawberry leaves
And over them spread;
And all the day long,
They sang them this song –
  Poor babes in the wood!
  Poor babes in the wood!
And won't you remember
  The babes in the wood?

Anon.

Counting-out Rhyme

Silver bark of beech, and sallow
Bark of yellow birch and yellow
  Twig of willow.

Stripe of green in moosewood maple,
Colour seen in leaf of apple,
  Bark of popple.

Wood of popple pale as moonbeam,
Wood of oak for yoke and barn-beam,
  Wood of hornbeam.

Silver bark of beech, and hollow
Stem of elder, tall and yellow
  Twig of willow.

Edna St. Vincent Millay (1892–1950)

barefoot

After that tight
Choke of sock
And blunt
Weight of shoe,

The foot can feel
Clover's green
Skin
Growing,

And the fine
Invisible
Teeth
Of gentle grass,

And the cool
Breath
Of the earth
Beneath.

Valerie Worth (1935–)

The Owl

Downhill I came, hungry, and yet not starved;
Cold, yet had heat within me that was proof
Against the North wind; tired, yet so that rest
Had seemed the sweetest thing under a roof.

Then at the inn I had food, fire, and rest,
Knowing how hungry, cold, and tired was I.
All of the night was quite barred out except
An owl's cry, a most melancholy cry

Shaken out long and clear upon the hill,
No merry note, nor cause of merriment,
But one telling me plain what I escaped
And others could not, that night, as in I went.

And salted was my food, and my repose,
Salted and sobered, too, by the bird's voice
Speaking for all who lay under the stars,
Soldiers and poor, unable to rejoice.

Edward Thomas (1878–1917)

Where the Bee Sucks

(extract from The Tempest)
Where the bee sucks, there suck I:
In a cowslip's bell I lie;
There I couch when owls do cry.
On the bat's back I do fly
After summer merrily.
Merrily, merrily shall I live now
Under the blossom that
    hangs on the bough.

William Shakespeare
(1564–1616)

From a Railway Carriage

Faster than fairies, faster than witches,
Bridges and houses, hedges and ditches;
And charging along like troops in a battle,
All through the meadows the horses and cattle;
All of the sights of the hill and the plain
Fly as thick as driving rain;
And ever again, in the wink of an eye,
Painted stations whistle by.

Here is a child who clambers and scrambles,
All by himself and gathering brambles;
Here is a tramp who stands and gazes;
And there is the green for stringing the daisies!
Here is a cart run away in the road
Lumping along with man and load;
And here is a mill, and there is a river:
Each a glimpse and gone for ever!

R. L. Stevenson (1850–1894)

Tramp

A knock at the door
And he stands there,
A tramp with his can
Asking for tea,
Strong for a poor man
On his way – where?

He looks at his feet,
I look at the sky;
Over us the planes build
The shifting rafters
Of that new world
We have sworn by.

I sleep in my bed,
He sleeps in the old,
Dead leaves of a ditch.
My dreams are haunted;
Are his dreams rich?
If I wake early,
He wakes cold.

R. S. Thomas (1913–)

I Wandered Lonely as a Cloud

I wandered lonely as a cloud
That floats on high o'er vales and hills,
When all at once I saw a crowd,
A host, of golden daffodils;
Beside the lake, beneath the trees,
Fluttering and dancing in the breeze.

Continuous as the stars that shine
And twinkle on the milky way,
They stretched in never-ending line
Along the margin of a bay:
Ten thousand saw I at a glance,
Tossing their heads in sprightly dance.

The waves beside them danced; but they
Out-did the sparkling waves in glee:
A poet could not but be gay,
In such a jocund company:
I gazed – and gazed – but little thought
What wealth the show to me had brought:

For oft, when on my couch I lie
In vacant or in pensive mood,
They flash upon that inward eye
Which is the bliss of solitude;
And then my heart with pleasure fills
And dances with the daffodils.

William Wordsworth (1770–1850)

What is Pink?

What is pink? A rose is pink
By the fountain's brink.
What is red? A poppy's red
In its barley bed.
What is blue? The sky is blue
Where the clouds float through.
What is white? A swan is white
Sailing in the light.
What is yellow? Pears are yellow,
Rich and ripe and mellow.
What is green? The grass is green,
With small flowers between.
What is violet? Clouds are violet
In the summer twilight.
What is orange? Why, an orange,
Just an orange!

Christina Rossetti (1830–1895)

Beech Leaves

In autumn down the beechwood path
The leaves lie thick upon the ground.
It's there I love to kick my way
And hear their crisp and crashing sound.

I am a giant, and my steps
Echo and thunder to the sky.
How the small creatures of the woods
Must quake and cower as I pass by!

This brave and merry noise I make
In summer also when I stride
Down to the shining, pebbly sea
And kick the frothing waves aside.

James Reeves (1909–1978)

in Just-

in Just-
spring   when the world is mud-
luscious the little
lame balloonman

whistles   far   and wee

and eddieandbill come
running from marbles and
piracies and it's
spring

when the world is puddle-wonderful

the queer
old balloonman whistles
far   and   wee
and bettyandisbel come dancing

from hop-scotch and jump-rope and

it's
spring
and
    the
        goat-footed

balloonMan   whistles
far
and
wee

      E. E. Cummings (1894–1962)

Isn't it Amazing?

Now isn't it amazing
That seeds grow into flowers,
That grubs become bright butterflies
And rainbows come from showers,
That busy bees make honey gold
And never spend time lazing,
That eggs turn into singing birds,
Now isn't that amazing?

Max Fatchen (1920–)

Rain in Summer

How beautiful is the rain!
After the dust and heat,
In the broad and fiery street,
In the narrow lane,
How beautiful is the rain!

How it clatters along the roofs,
Like the tramp of hoofs!
How it gushes and struggles out
From the throat of the
overflowing spout!
Across the window pane
It pours and pours;
And swift and wide,
With a muddy tide,
Like a river down the gutter roars
The rain, the welcome rain!

H. W. Longfellow (1807–1882)

The Lonely Scarecrow

My poor old bones – I've only two –
A broomshank and a broken stave,
My ragged gloves are a disgrace,
My one peg-foot is in the grave.

I wear the labourer's old clothes;
Coat, shirt and trousers all undone.
I bear my cross upon a hill
In rain and shine, in snow and sun.

I cannot help the way I look.
My funny hat is full of hay.
– O, wild birds, come and nest in me!
Why do you always fly away?

James Kirkup (1923–)

A Boy's Song

Where the pools are bright and deep,
Where the grey trout lies asleep,
Up the river and over the lea,
That's the way for Billy and me.

Where the blackbird sings the latest,
Where the hawthorn blooms the sweetest,
Where the nestlings chirp and flee,
That's the way for Billy and me.

Where the mowers mow the cleanest,
Where the hay lies thick and greenest,
There to track the homeward bee,
That's the way for Billy and me.

Where the hazel bank is steepest,
Where the shadow falls the deepest,
Where the clustering nuts fall free,
That's the way for Billy and me.

Why the boys should drive away
Little sweet maidens from the play,
Or love to banter and fight so well,
That's the thing I never could tell.

But this I know, I love to play
Through the meadow, among the hay;
Up the water and over the lea,
That's the way for Billy and me.

James Hogg (1770–1835)

Not a Very Cheerful Song, I'm Afraid

There was a gloomy lady,
With a gloomy duck and a gloomy drake,
And they all three wandered gloomily,
Beside a gloomy lake,
On a gloomy, gloomy, gloomy, gloomy, gloomy, gloomy day.

Now underneath that gloomy lake
The gloomy lady's gone.
But the gloomy duck and the gloomy drake
Swim on and on and on,
On a gloomy, gloomy, gloomy, gloomy, gloomy, gloomy day.

Adrian Mitchell (1932–)

Tree

From the depths of my roots
to the tips of my leaves,
I am tree. I am tree. I am tree.
I am evergreen deciduous coniferous
massive Oak and mini Bonsai.
I am Rowan and I am Silver Birch.
Beech – or, if you prefer, *Fagus Sylvatica*.
Call me what you will, Man.
It makes no difference to me.
I am tree. I am tree. I am tree.

Do you like me? Do you like my trunk?
What does it remind you of?
An elephant's foot? A massive rope of wood?
What about my bark? Does it make you think
of a rhino's horn? The scales of fish?
And satin? And silk? What else?
My skins are as various as my names.
What do you make of my branches?
The bare, slender arms of a girl, maybe?
But with an old woman's elbows.
In her gnarled arthritic fingers
she clasps the nests of birds.
How do you feel about my roots?
Do they seem to wriggle, to writhe?
They've been mistaken for snakes.
And what about my fruit?
Is it still forbidden to you?
Who forbade it? I didn't.

I am root. Branch. Leaf. Sap.
Bark. Blossom. Bud. I am tree.
Without me a flat horizon would be
a flat horizon.

When you look at me, Man, you see
fuel, timber, a table, pulp, paper –
would you make a book out of me?
But it would not have leaves like these.

I am older than you, Man.
I was there in your garden of Eden,
and before: my roots go deeper than you know,
deep into your heart and deeper still.
They clasp the bones of your ancestors
and go deeper yet. I mean more to you
than you know, Man. Why else
would you carve your hearts in me?
Your saws and your axes
    will not fell me.
Don't underestimate me.
    I'll outlive you.

Come and sit in the cool shade of my bole.
Beneath the thatched roof of my branches.
Lean against my bark, close your eyes.
Breathe deeply. Now, feel what I am.
I am tree. I am tree. I am tree.

Brian McCabe (1951–)

The Brook

(extract)

I come from haunts of coot and hern,
 I make a sudden sally
And sparkle out among the fern,
 To bicker down a valley.

By thirty hills I hurry down,
 Or slip between the ridges,
By twenty thorps, a little town,
 And half a hundred bridges.

Till last by Philip's farm I flow
 To join the brimming river,
For men may come and men may go,
 But I go on for ever.

I chatter over stony ways,
 In little sharps and trebles,
I bubble into eddying bays,
 I babble on the pebbles.

With many a curve my banks I fret
 By many a field and fallow,
And many a fairy foreland set
 With willow-weed and mallow.

I chatter, chatter, as I flow
 To join the brimming river,
For men may come and men may go,
 But I go on for ever.

  Alfred, Lord Tennyson (1809–1892)

FOOD & FUN

'Spaghetti! Spaghetti!'

A Fox Started Out in a Hungry Plight

A fox started out in a hungry plight,
And begged of the moon to give him light,
For he'd a long way to go that night
Before he could reach the downs, O!
Downs, O! Downs, O!
For he'd a long way to go that night
Before he could reach the downs, O!

The Fox when he came to the farmer's gate,
What should he see but the farmer's black duck!
'I love you,' says he, 'for your master's sake,
And I long to be picking your bones, O!
Bones, O! Bones, O!
I love you,' says he, 'for your master's sake,
And I long to be picking your bones, O!'

Then he seized the black duck by the neck,
And swung her all across his back,
The black duck cried out, 'Quack! Quack! Quack!'
With her legs hanging dangling down, O!
Down, O! Down, O!
The black duck cried out, 'Quack! Quack! Quack!'
With her legs hanging dangling down, O!

Old Mother Slipper-slopper
    jumped out of bed,
And out of the window she
    popped her old head,
Crying, 'John, John, John,
    the black duck is gone,
And the Fox has run off
    to his den, O!
Den, O! Den, O!
John, John, John,
    the black duck is gone,
And the Fox has run off
    to his den, O!'

Then John, he went up to the top of the hill,
And blew his horn both loud and shrill.
Says the Fox, 'That is very pretty music, still
I'd rather be safe in my den, O!
Den, O! Den, O!'
Says the Fox, 'That is very pretty music, still
I'd rather be safe in my den, O!'

At last Mr Fox got home to his den,
To his dear little foxes, eight, nine, ten,
Says he, 'We're in luck, here's a fine fat duck,
With her legs all dangling down, O!
Down, O! Down, O!'
Says he, 'We're in luck, here's a fine fat duck,
With her legs all dangling down, O!'

Then the Fox sat down with his cubs and his wife;
They did very well without fork and knife,
Nor ate a better duck in all their life,
And the little ones picked the bones, O!
Bones, O! Bones, O!
They never ate a better duck in all their life,
And the little ones picked the bones, O!

Anon.

Beautiful Soup

Beautiful Soup, so rich and green,
  Waiting in a hot tureen!
Who for such dainties would not stoop?
Soup of the evening, beautiful Soup!
Soup of the evening, beautiful Soup!
  Beau-ootiful Soo-oop!
  Beau-ootiful Soo-oop!
Soo-oop of the e-e-evening,
  Beautiful, beautiful Soup!

Beautiful Soup! Who cares for fish,
  Game, or any other dish?
Who would not give all else for two p
ennyworth only of beautiful Soup?
Pennyworth only of beautiful Soup?
  Beau-ootiful Soo-oop!
  Beau-ootiful Soo-oop!
Soo-oop of the e-e-evening,
  Beautiful, beauti-FUL SOUP!

Lewis Carroll (1832–1898)

Calico Pie

Calico Pie,
The little Birds fly
Down to the calico tree,
Their wings were blue,
And they sang 'Tilly-loo!'
Till away they flew, –
And they never came back to me!
They never came back!
They never came back!
They never came back to me!

Calico Jam,
The little Fish swam,
Over the syllabub sea,
He took off his hat,
To the Sole and the Sprat,
And the Willeby-wat, –
But he never came back to me!
He never came back!
He never came back!
He never came back to me!

Calico Ban,
The little Mice ran,
To be ready in time for tea,
Flippity flup,
They drank it all up,
And danced in the cup, –
But they never came back to me!
They never came back!
They never came back!
They never came back to me!

Calico Drum,
The Grasshoppers come,
The Butterfly, Beetle, and Bee,
Over the ground,
Around and round,
With a hop and a bound, –
But they never came back!
They never came back!
They never came back!
They never came back to me!

Edward Lear (1812–1888)

This Is Just to Say

I have eaten
the plums
that were in
the icebox

and which
you were probably
saving
for breakfast

Forgive me
they were delicious
so sweet
and so cold

William Carlos Williams (1883–1963)

The Story of Augustus who Would Not have Any Soup

Augustus was a chubby lad;
Fat ruddy cheeks Augustus had:
And everybody saw with joy
The plump and hearty, healthy boy.
He ate and drank as he was told,
And never let his soup get cold.
But one day, one cold winter's day,
He screamed out 'Take the soup away!
O take the nasty soup away!
I won't have any soup today.'

Next day, now look, the picture shows
How lank and lean Augustus grows!
Yet, though he feels so weak and ill,
The naughty fellow cries out still
'Not any soup for me, I say:
O take the nasty soup away!
I *won't* have any soup today.'

The third day comes: Oh what a sin!
To make himself so pale and thin.
Yet, when the soup is put on table,
He screams, as loud as he is able,
'Not any soup for me, I say:
O take the nasty soup away!
I WON'T have any soup today.'

Look at him, now the fourth day's come!
He scarcely weighs a sugar-plum;
He's like a little bit of thread,
And, on the fifth day, he was – dead!

Heinrich Hoffmann (1809–1894)

No Peas for the Wicked

No peas for the wicked
No carrots for the damned
No parsnips for the naughty
    O Lord we pray

No sprouts for the shameless
No cabbage for the shady
No lettuce for the lecherous
    No way, no way

No potatoes for the deviants
No radish for the riff-raff
No spinach for the spineless
    Lock them away

No beetroot for the boasters
No mange-tout for the mobsters
No corn-on-the-cob et cetera
    (Shall we call it a day?)

Roger McGough (1937–)

I Eat my Peas with Honey

I eat my peas with honey;
I've done it all my life.
It makes the peas taste funny,
But it keeps them on the knife.

Anon.

The African Lion

To meet a bad lad on the African waste
Is a thing that a lion enjoys;
But he rightly and strongly objects to the taste
Of good and uneatable boys.

When he bites off a piece of a boy of that sort
He spits it right out of his mouth,
And retires with a loud and dissatisfied snort
To the east, or the west, or the south.

So lads of good habits, on coming across
A lion, need feel no alarm,
For they know they are sure
   to escape with the loss
Of a leg, or a head,
   or an arm.

A. E. Housman
(1859–1936)

Spaghetti! Spaghetti!

Spaghetti! spaghetti!
you're wonderful stuff,
I love you, spaghetti,
I can't get enough.
You're covered with sauce
and you're sprinkled with cheese,
spaghetti! spaghetti!
oh, give me some more please.

Spaghetti! spaghetti!
piled high in a mound,
you wiggle, you wriggle,
you squiggle around.
There's slurpy spaghetti
all over my plate,
spaghetti! spaghetti!
I think you are great.

Spaghetti! spaghetti!
I love you a lot,
you're slishy, you're sloshy,
delicious and hot.
I gobble you down
oh, I can't get enough,
spaghetti! spaghetti!
you're wonderful stuff.

Jack Prelutsky (1940–)

The Worm

When the earth is turned in spring
The worms are fat as anything.

And birds come flying all around
To eat the worms right off the ground.

They like worms just as much as I
Like bread and milk and apple pie.

And once, when I was very young,
I put a worm right on my tongue.

I didn't like the taste a bit,
And so I didn't swallow it.

But oh, it makes my Mother squirm
Because she *thinks* I ate that worm!

Ralph Bergengren

The King's Breakfast

The King asked
The Queen, and
The Queen asked
The Dairymaid:
'Could we have some butter for
The Royal slice of bread?'
The Queen asked
The Dairymaid,
The Dairymaid
Said, 'Certainly,
I'll go and tell
The cow
Now
Before she goes to bed.'
The Dairymaid
She curtsied,
And went and told
The Alderney:
'Don't forget the butter for
The Royal slice of bread.'
The Alderney
Said sleepily:
'You'd better tell
His Majesty
That many people nowadays
Like marmalade
Instead.'

The Dairymaid
Said, 'Fancy!'
And went to
Her Majesty.
She curtsied to the Queen, and
She turned a little red:
'Excuse me,
Your Majesty,
For taking of
The liberty,
But marmalade is tasty, if
It's very
Thickly
Spread.'

The Queen said
'Oh!'
And went to
His Majesty:
'Talking of the butter for
The royal slice of bread,
Many people
Think that
Marmalade
Is nicer.
Would you like to try a little
Marmalade
Instead?'

The King said,
'Bother!'
And then he said,
'Oh, deary me!'
The King sobbed, 'Oh, deary me!'
And went back to bed.
'Nobody,'
He whimpered,
'Could call me
A fussy man;
I *only* want
A little bit
Of butter for
My bread!'

The Queen said,
'There, there!'
And went to
The Dairymaid.
The Dairymaid
Said, 'There, there!'
And went to the shed.
The cow said,
'There, there!
I didn't really
Mean it;
Here's milk for his porringer.
And butter for his bread.'

The Queen took
The butter
And brought it to
His Majesty;
The King said,
'Butter, eh?'
And bounced out of bed.
'Nobody,' he said,
As he kissed her
Tenderly,
'Nobody,' he said,
As he slid down
The banisters,
'Nobody,
My darling,
Could call me
A fussy man –
BUT
I do like a little bit of butter to my bread!'

A. A. Milne (1882–1956)

The Comic Adventures
of Old Mother Hubbard and Her Dog

Old Mother Hubbard
Went to the cupboard,
To give the poor dog a bone;
When she came there
The cupboard was bare,
And so the poor dog had none.

She went to the baker's
To buy him some bread;
When she came back
The dog was dead.

She went to the undertaker's
To buy him a coffin;
When she came back
The dog was laughing.

She took a clean dish
To get him some tripe;
When she came back
He was smoking his pipe.

She went to the alehouse
  To get him some beer;
When she came back
  The dog sat in a chair.

She went to the tavern
  For white wine and red;
When she came back
  The dog stood on his head.

She went to the fruiterer's
  To buy him some fruit;
When she came back
  He was playing the flute.

She went to the tailor's
  To buy him a coat;
When she came back
  He was riding a goat.

She went to the hatter's
  To buy him a hat;
When she came back
  He was feeding the cat.

She went to the barber's
  To buy him a wig;
When she came back
  He was dancing a jig.

She went to the cobbler's
  To buy him some shoes;
When she came back
  He was reading the news.

She went to the seamstress
  To buy him some linen;
When she came back
  The dog was spinning.

She went to the hosier's
  To buy him some hose;
When she came back
  He was dressed in his clothes.

The dame made a curtsy,
  The dog made a bow;
The dame said 'Your Servant',
  The dog said 'Bow-wow'.

Sarah Catherine Martin
(1768–1826)

Blackberry-Picking

For Philip Hobsbaum

Late August, given heavy rain and sun
For a full week, the blackberries would ripen.
At first, just one, a glossy purple clot
Among others, red, green, hard as a knot.
You ate that first one and its flesh was sweet
Like thickened wine: summer's blood was in it
Leaving stains upon the tongue and lust for
Picking. Then red ones inked up and that hunger
Sent us out with milk-cans, pea-tins, jam-pots
Where briars scratched and wet grass bleached our boots.
Round hayfields, cornfields and potato-drills
We trekked and picked until the cans were full,
Until the tinkling bottom had been covered
With green ones, and on top big dark blobs burned
Like a plate of eyes. Our hands were peppered
With thorn pricks, our palms sticky as Bluebeard's.

We hoarded the fresh berries in the byre.
But when the bath was filled we found a fur,
A rat-grey fungus, glutting on our cache.
The juice was stinking too. Once off the bush
The fruit fermented, the sweet flesh would turn sour.
I always felt like crying. It wasn't fair
That all the lovely canfuls smelt of rot.
Each year I hoped they'd keep, knew they would not.

Seamus Heaney (1939–)

Kindness to Animals

If I went vegetarian
And didn't eat lambs for dinner,
I think I'd be a better person
And also thinner.

But the lamb is not endangered
And at least I can truthfully say
I have never, ever eaten a barn owl,
So perhaps I am OK.

Wendy Cope (1945–)

'Mary had a little lamb'

Mary had a little lamb,
A lobster, and some prunes,
A glass of milk, a piece of pie,
And then some macaroons.

It made the busy waiters grin
To see her order so,
And when they carried Mary out,
Her face was white as snow.

Anon.

BALLADS
& STORIES

*'And people call me
the Pied Piper'*

Young Beichan

In London was Young Beichan born,
He long'd strange countries for to see;
But he was ta'en by a savage Moor
Who handled him right cruellie.

For he view'd the fashions of that land,
Their way of worship viewèd he;
But to Mahound or Termagant
Would Beichan never bend a knee.

So thro' every shoulder they've bored a bore,
And thro' every bore they've putten a tree,
And they have made him trail the wine
And spices on his fair bodie.

They've casten him in a dungeon deep,
Where he could neither hear nor see;
And fed him on nought but bread and water
Till he for hunger's like to die.

This Moor he had but ae daughter,
Her name was callèd Susie Pye,
And every day as she took the air
She heard Young Beichan sadly crie:

'My hounds they all run masterless,
My hawks they flie from tree to tree,
My youngest brother will heir my lands;
Fair England again I'll never see!

'O were I free as I hae been,
And my ship swimming once more on sea,
I'd turn my face to fair England
And sail no more to a strange countrie!'

Young Beichan's song for thinking on
All night she never closed her e'e;
She's stown† the keys from her father's head   †stolen
Wi' mickle gold and white monie.

And she has open'd the prison doors:
I wot she open'd twa or three
Ere she could come Young Beichan at,
He was lock'd up so curiouslie.

'O hae ye any lands or rents,
Or cities in your own countrie,
Cou'd free you out of prison strong
And cou'd maintain a lady free?' –

'O London city is my own,
And other cities twa or three;
I'll give them all to the lady fair
That out of prison will set me free.'

O she has bribed her father's men
Wi' mickle gold and white monie,
She's gotten the key's of the prison strong,
And she has set Young Beichan free.

She's fed him upon the good spice-cake,
The Spanish wine and the malvoisie;
She's broken a ring from off her finger
And to Beichan half of it gave she.

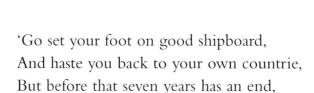

'Go set your foot on good shipboard,
And haste you back to your own countrie,
But before that seven years has an end,
Come back again, love, and marry me.'

It was long or seven years had an end
She long'd full sore her love to see;
So she's set her foot on good ship-board
And turn'd her back on her own countrie.

She's sailèd east, she's sailèd west,
She's sailèd all across the sea,
And when she came to fair England
The bells were ringing merrilie.

'O whose are a' yon flock o' sheep?
And whose are a' yon flock o' kye?†   †cattle
And whose are a' yon pretty castles,
That I so often do pass by?'

'O they are a' Lord Beichan's sheep,
And they are a' Lord Beichan's kye,
And they are a' Lord Beichan's castles
That you so often do pass by.

'O there's a wedding in yonder ha',
Has lasted thirty days and three;
Lord Beichan will not bed wi' his bride
For love of one that's 'yond the sea.'

When she came to Young Beichan's gate
She tirlèd† softly at the pin;   †rattled
So ready was the proud portèr
To open and let this lady in.

'Is this Young Beichan's gates?' she says,
'Or is that noble lord within?' –
'He's up the stairs wi' his bonny bride,
For this is the day o' his weddin'.' –

'O has he taken a bonny bride,
And has he clean forgotton me?'
And sighing said that ladye gay,
'I wish I were in my own countrie!'

She's putten her hand in her pockèt
And gi'en the porter guineas three;
Says, 'Take ye that, ye proud portèr,
And bid the bridegroom speak with me.'

And she has ta'en her gay gold ring,
That with her love she brake so free;
Says, 'Gie him that, ye proud portèr,
And bid the bridegroom speak with me.'

O when the porter came up the stair,
He's kneelèd low upon his knee:
'Won up†, won up, ye proud portèr,   †get
And what makes a' this courtesie?' –

'O I've been porter at your gates
I'm sure this thirty years and three,
But there is a lady stands thereat
The fairest I did ever see.'

It's out then spake the bride's mother,
– Aye, and an angry woman as she –
'Ye might have excepted our bonny bride,
And twa or three of our companie.'

'My dame, your daughter's fair enough,
And aye the fairer mote she be!
But the fairest time that ever she was,
She'll no compare wi' this ladye.

'For on every finger she has a ring,
And on the mid-finger she has three,
And as mickle gold she has on her brow
'Would buy an earldome o' land to me.

'And this golden ring that's broken in twa,
She sends the half o' this golden ring,
And bids you speak with a lady fair,
That out o' prison did you bring.'

Then up and started Young Beichan,
And sware so loud by Our Ladye,
'It can be none by Susie Pye,
That has come over the sea to me!'

O quickly ran he down the stair,
Of fifteen steps he made but three;
He's ta'en his bonny love in his arms
And kiss'd and kiss'd her tenderlie.

'O have ye ta'en another bride,
And have ye quite forsaken me?
And have ye clean forgotten her
That gave you life and libertie?'

She's lookèd over her left shoulder
To hide the tears stood in her e'e;
'Now fare-thee-well, Young Beichan,' she says –
'I'll strive to think no more on thee.'

'O never, never, Susie Pye,
For surely this can never be,
That ever I shall wed but her
That's done and dreed[†] so much for me!'   [†]suffered

Then up bespake the bride's mother –
She never was heard to speak so free:
'Ye'll not forsake my only daughter,
Though Susie Pye has cross'd the sea.'

'Take home, take home your daughter, madam,
She's never a bit the worse for me;
For saving a kiss of her bonny lips
Of your daughter's body I am free.'

He's ta'en her by the milk-white hand
And led her to yon fountain-stone;[†]   [†]font
He's changed her name from Susie Pye
And call'd her his bonny love Lady Joan.

                              Anon.

The Death and Burial of Cock Robin

Who killed Cock Robin?
  I, said the Sparrow,
  With my bow and arrow,
I killed Cock Robin.

Who saw him die?
  I, said the Fly,
  With my little eye,
I saw him die.

Who caught his blood?
  I, said the Fish,
  With my little dish,
I caught his blood.

Who'll make his shroud?
  I, said the Beetle,
  With my thread and needle,
I'll make his shroud.

Who'll dig his grave?
  I, said the Owl,
  With my pick and shovel,
I'll dig his grave.

Who'll be the parson?
  I, said the Rook,
  With my little book,
I'll be the parson.

Who'll be the clerk?
  I, said the Lark,
  If it's not in the dark,
I'll be the clerk.

Who'll carry the link?
  I, said the Linnet,
  I'll fetch it in a minute,
I'll carry the link.

Who'll be the chief mourner?
  I, said the Dove,
  I mourn for my love,
I'll be chief mourner.

Who'll carry the coffin?
  I, said the Kite,
  If it's not through the night,
I'll carry the coffin.

Who'll bear the pall?
  We, said the Wren,
  Both the cock and the hen,
We'll bear the pall.

Who'll sing the psalm?
  I, said the Thrush,
  As she sat on a bush,
I'll sing a psalm.

Who'll toll the bell?
  I, said the Bull,
  Because I can pull,
So Cock Robin, farewell.

All the birds of the air
  Fell a-sighing and a-sobbing,
  When they heard the bell toll
For poor Cock Robin.

Anon.

Children's Crusade

In 'thirty-nine in Poland
There was a bloody fight
And many a town and village
Turned to waste land overnight.

Sisters lost their brothers
Wives were widowed by the war
And in fire and desolation
Children found their kin no more.

There came no news from Poland
Neither letter nor printed word
But in an eastern country
A curious tale is heard.

Snow fell, as they related
In a certain eastern town
How a new crusade of children
In Poland had begun.

For all along the highways
Troops of hungry children roamed
And gathered to them others
Who stood by ruined homes.

They wished to flee the slaughter
For the nightmare did not cease
And some day reach a country
Where there was peace.

They had a little leader
To show them where to go.
Yet he was sorely troubled
Since the way he did not know.

A girl of ten was carrying
A little child of four.
All she lacked to be a mother
Was a country without war.

In a coat with a velvet collar
A little Jew was dressed
He had been reared on whitest bread
But he marched on with the rest.

There was a thin and wretched boy
Who held himself apart.
That he came from a Nazi legation
Was a load of guilt in his heart.

They also had a dog with them
Which they had caught for food.
They spared it; so, another mouth
It followed where it would.

There was a school for penmanship
And teaching did not cease.
On the broken side of a tank
They learned to spell out *peace*.

A girl of twelve, a boy of fifteen
Had a love affair
And in a ruined farmyard
She sat and combed his hair.

But love could not endure
Cold wind began to blow:
And how can saplings bloom
When covered deep in snow?

They had a funeral besides
Two Poles and two Germans carried
The boy with the velvet collar
To the place where he was buried.

There were Catholics and Protestants
And Nazis at the grave
At the end a little Communist spoke
Of the future the living have.

So there was faith and hope
But lack of bread and meat.
And if they stole let no one blame
Who never bade them eat.

Let no one blame the poor man
Who never asked them in
For many have the will but have
No flour in the bin.

They strove to travel southward.
The south is where, 'tis said
At high noon the sun stands
Directly overhead.

They found a wounded soldier
In a pinewood one day.
And for a week they tended him
In hopes he'd know the way.

To Bilgoray, he said to them.
The fever made him rave.
Upon the eighth day he died.
They laid him in his grave.

Sometimes there were signposts
Though covered up in snow
All turned around and pointing wrong
But this they did not know.

And no grim joke it was, but done
On military grounds.
And long they sought for Bilgoray
Which never could be found.

They stood about their leader
Who stared at the snowy sky.
He pointed with his finger
Saying: Yonder it must lie.

Once, at night, they saw a fire
They turned away in fear.
Once three tanks came rolling by
Which meant that men were near.

Once, when they reached a city
They veered and went around.
They travelled then by night alone
Till they had passed the town.

Towards what was south-east Poland
In deeply drifting snow
The five and fifty children
Were last seen to go.

And if I close my eyes
I see them wander on
From one ruined barnyard
To another one.

Above them in the clouds I see
A new and greater host
Wearily breasting the cold wind
Homeless and lost

Seeking for a land of peace
Without the crash and flame of war
That scars the soil from which they came
And this host is always more.

Now in the gloom it seems to me
They come from many other places:
In the changing clouds I see
Spanish, French, yellow faces.

In January of that year
Poles caught a hungry dog
Around whose neck a placard hung
'Twas tied there with a cord.

These words thereon were: Please send help!
We don't know where we are.
We are five and fifty
The dog will lead you here.

And if you cannot come to us
Please drive him out.
Don't shoot the dog for no one else
Can find the spot.

A childish hand had written
The words the peasants read.
Since that time two years have passed.
The starving dog is dead.

Bertold Brecht (1898–1956)
translated from the German

Matilda

who told lies, and was burned to death

Matilda told such Dreadful Lies,
It made one Gasp and Stretch one's Eyes;
Her Aunt, who, from her Earliest Youth,
Had kept a Strict Regard for Truth,
Attempted to Believe Matilda:
The effort very nearly killed her,
And would have done so, had not She
Discovered this Infirmity.
For once, towards the Close of Day,
Matilda, growing tired of play,
And finding she was left alone,
Went tiptoe to the Telephone
And summoned the Immediate Aid
Of London's Noble Fire-Brigade.
Within an hour the Gallant Band
Were pouring in on every hand,
From Putney, Hackney
    Downs and Bow,
With Courage high and
    Hearts a-glow
They galloped, roaring
    through the Town,
'Matilda's House is
    Burning Down!'
Inspired by British
    Cheers and Loud
Proceeding from the
    Frenzied Crowd,

They ran their ladders through a score
Of windows on the Ball Room Floor;
And took Peculiar Pains to Souse
The Pictures up and down the House,
Until Matilda's Aunt succeeded
In showing them they were not needed
And even then she had to pay
To get the Men to go away!

It happened that a few Weeks later
Her Aunt was off to the Theatre
To see that Interesting Play
The Second Mrs Tanqueray.
She had refused to take her Niece
To hear this Entertaining Piece:
A Deprivation Just and Wise
To Punish her for Telling Lies.
That Night a Fire *did* break out –
You should have heard Matilda Shout!
You should have heard her Scream and Bawl,
And throw the window up and call
To People passing in the Street –
(The rapidly increasing Heat
Encouraging her to obtain
Their confidence) – but all in vain!
For every time She shouted 'Fire!'
They only answered 'Little Liar!'
And therefore when her Aunt returned,
Matilda, and the House, were Burned.

Hilaire Belloc (1870–1953)

The Pied Piper of Hamelin

Hamelin Town's in Brunswick,
By famous Hanover city;
The river Weser, deep and wide,
Washes its wall on the southern side;
A pleasanter spot you never spied;
But, when begins my ditty,
Almost five hundred years ago,
To see the townsfolk suffer so
From vermin, was a pity.

Rats!
They fought the dogs, and killed the cats,
And bit the babies in the cradles,
And ate the cheeses out of the vats,
And licked the soup from the cooks' own ladles,
Split open the kegs of salted sprats,
Made nests inside men's Sunday hats,

And even spoiled the women's chats,
By drowning their speaking
With shrieking and squeaking
In fifty different sharps and flats.

At last the people in a body
To the Town Hall came flocking:
"'Tis clear,' cried they, 'our Mayor's a noddy;
And as for our Corporation – shocking
To think we buy gowns lined with ermine
For dolts that can't or won't determine
What's best to rid us of our vermin!
You hope, because you're old and obese,
To find in the furry civic robe ease?
Rouse up, Sirs! Give your brains a racking,
To find the remedy we're lacking,
Or, sure as fate, we'll send you packing!'
At this the Mayor and Corporation
Quaked with a mighty consternation.

An hour they sate in council,
At length the Mayor broke silence:
'For a guilder I'd my ermine gown sell;
I wish I were a mile hence!
It's easy to bid one rack one's brain –
I'm sure my poor head aches again
I've scratched it so, and all in vain.
Oh for a trap, a trap, a trap!'
Just as he said this, what should hap
At the chamber door but a gentle tap?
'Bless us,' cried the Mayor, 'what's that?'
(With the Corporation as he sat,

Looking little though wondrous fat;
Nor brighter was his eye, nor moister
Than a too-long-opened oyster,
Save when at noon his paunch grew mutinous
For a plate of turtle green and glutinous)
'Only a scraping of shoes on the mat?
Anything like the sound of a rat
Makes my heart go pit-a-pat!'

'Come in!' – the Mayor cried, looking bigger:
And in did come the strangest figure!
His queer long coat from heel to head
Was half of yellow and half of red;
And he himself was tall and thin,
With sharp blue eyes, each like a pin,
And light loose hair, yet swarthy skin,
No tuft on cheek nor beard on chin,
But lips where smiles went out and in –
There was no guessing his kith and kin!
And nobody could enough admire
The tall man and his quaint attire:
Quoth one: 'It's as my great-grandsire,
Starting up at the Trump of Doom's tone,
Had walked this way from his painted tomb-stone!'

He advanced to the council-table:
And, 'Please your honours,' said he, 'I'm able
By means of a secret charm to draw
All creatures living beneath the sun,
That creep or swim or fly or run,
After me so as you never saw!

And I chiefly use my charm
On creatures that do people harm,
The mole and toad and newt and viper;
And people call me the Pied Piper.'
(And here they noticed round his neck
A scarf of red and yellow stripe,
To match with his coat of the self-same cheque;
And at the scarf's end hung a pipe;
And his fingers, they noticed, were ever straying
As if impatient to be playing
Upon this pipe, as low it dangled
Over his vesture so old-fangled.)
'Yet,' said he, 'poor piper as I am,
In Tartary I freed the Cham,
Last June, from his huge swarms of gnats;
I eased in Asia the Nizam
Of a monstrous brood of vampyre-bats;
And as for what your brain bewilders,
If I can rid your town of rats
Will you give me a thousand guilders?'
'One? fifty thousand!' – was the exclamation
Of the astonished Mayor and Corporation.

Into the street the Piper stept,
Smiling first a little smile,
As if he knew what magic slept
In his quiet pipe the while;
Then, like a musical adept,
To blow the pipe his lips he wrinkled,
And green and blue his sharp eyes twinkled
Like à candle-flame where salt is sprinkled;

And ere three shrill notes the pipe uttered,
You heard as if an army muttered;
And the muttering grew to a grumbling;
And the grumbling grew to a mighty rumbling;
And out of the houses the rats came tumbling.

Great rats, small rats, lean rats, brawny rats,
Brown rats, black rats, grey rats, tawny rats,
Grave old plodders, gay young friskers,
Fathers, mothers, uncles, cousins,
Cocking tails and pricking whiskers,
Families by tens and dozens,
Brothers, sisters, husbands, wives –
Followed the Piper for their lives.
From street to street he piped advancing,
And step for step they followed dancing,
Until they came to the river Weser
Wherein all plunged and perished!
– Save one who, stout as Julius Caesar,
Swam across and lived to carry
(As he, the manuscript he cherished)
To Rat-land home his commentary:
Which was, 'At the first shrill notes of the pipe,
I heard a sound as of scraping tripe,
And putting apples, wondrous ripe,
Into a cider-press's gripe:
And a moving away of pickle-tub boards,
And a leaving ajar of conserve-cupboards,
And a drawing the corks of train-oil flasks,
And a breaking the hoops of butter-casks;

And it seemed as if a voice
(Sweeter far than by harp or by psaltery
Is breathed) called out, Oh rats, rejoice!
The world is grown to one vast dry-saltery!
So, munch on, crunch on, take your nuncheon,
Breakfast, supper, dinner, luncheon!
And just as a bulky sugar-puncheon,
All ready staved, like a great sun shone
Glorious scarce an inch before me,
Just as methought it said, Come, bore me!
– I found the Weser rolling o'er me.'

You should have heard the Hamelin people
Ringing the bells till they rocked the steeple.
'Go,' cried the Mayor, 'and get long poles!
Poke out the nests and block up the holes!
Consult with carpenters and builders,
And leave in our town not even a trace
Of the rats!' – when suddenly, up the face
Of the Piper perked in the market-place,
With a 'First, if you please, my thousand guilders!'

A thousand guilders! The Mayor looked blue;
So did the Corporation too.
For council dinners made rare havoc
With Claret, Moselle, Vin-de-Grave, Hock;
And half the money would replenish
Their cellar's biggest butt with Rhenish.
To pay this sum to a wandering fellow
With a gipsy coat of red and yellow!
'Beside,' quoth the Mayor with a knowing wink,
'Our business was done at the river's brink;

We saw with our eyes the vermin sink,
And what's dead can't come to life, I think.
So, friend, we're not the folks to shrink
From the duty of giving you something to drink,
And a matter of money to put in your poke;
But as for the guilders, what we spoke
Of them, as you very well know, was in joke.
Besides, our losses have made us thrifty.
A thousand guilders! Come, take fifty!'

The Piper's face fell, and he cried,
'No trifling! I can't wait. Beside,
I've promised to visit by dinner time
Bagdad, and accept the prime
Of the Head-Cook's pottage, all he's rich in,
For having left, in the Caliph's kitchen,
Of a nest of scorpions no survivor –
With him I proved no bargain-driver,
With you, don't think I'll bate a stiver!
And folks who put me in a passion
May find me pipe to another fashion.'
'How?' cried the Mayor, 'd'ye think I'll brook
Being worse treated than a Cook?
Insulted by a lazy ribald
With idle pipe and vesture piebald?
You threaten us, fellow? Do your worst,
Blow your pipe there till you burst!'

Once more he stept into the street;
And to his lips again
Laid his long pipe of smooth straight cane;
And ere he blew three notes (such sweet

Soft notes as yet musician's cunning
Never gave the enraptured air)
There was a rustling, that seemed like a bustling
Of merry crowd justling at pitching and hustling,
Small feet were pattering, wooden shoes clattering,
Little hands clapping and little tongues chattering,
And, like fowls in a farm-yard when barley is scattering,
Out came the children running.
All the little boys and girls,
With rosy cheeks and flaxen curls,
And sparkling eyes and teeth like pearls,
Tripping and skipping, ran merrily after
The wonderful music with shouting and laughter.

The Mayor was dumb, and the Council stood
As if they were changed into blocks of wood,
Unable to move a step, or cry
To the children merrily skipping by –
And could only follow with the eye
That joyous crowd at the Piper's back.
But how the Mayor was on the rack,
And the wretched Council's bosoms beat,
As the Piper turned from the High Street
To where the Weser rolled its waters
Right in the way of their sons and daughters!
However he turned from South to West,
And to Koppelberg Hill his steps addressed,
And after him the children pressed;
Great was the joy in every breast.
'He never can cross that mighty top!
He's forced to let the piping drop,
And we shall see our children stop!'

When, lo, as they reached the mountain's side,
A wondrous portal opened wide,
As if a cavern was suddenly hollowed;
And the Piper advanced and the children followed,
And when all were in to the very last,
The door in the mountain-side shut fast.
Did I say, all? No! One was lame,
And could not dance the whole of the way;
And in after years, if you would blame
His sadness, he was used to say, –
'It's dull in our town since my playmates left!
I can't forget that I'm bereft
Of all the pleasant sights they see,
Which the Piper also promised me.
For he led us, he said, to a joyous land,
Joining the town and just at hand,
Where waters gushed and fruit-trees grew,
And flowers put forth a fairer hue,
And everything was strange and new;
The sparrows were brighter than peacocks here,
And their dogs outran our fallow deer,
And honey-bees had lost their stings,
And horses were born with eagles' wings:
And just as I became assured
My lame foot would be speedily cured,
The music stopped and I stood still,
And found myself outside the Hill,
Left alone against my will,
To go now limping as before,
And never hear of that country more!'

Alas, alas for Hamelin!
There came into many a burgher's pate
A text which says, that Heaven's Gate
Opes to the Rich at as easy rate
As the needle's eye takes a camel in!
The Mayor sent East, West, North and South,
To offer the Piper, by word of mouth,
Wherever it was men's lot to find him,
Silver and gold to his heart's content,
If he'd only return the way he went,
And bring the children behind him.

But when they saw 'twas a lost endeavour,
And Piper and dancers were gone for ever,
They made a decree that lawyers never
Should think their records dated duly
If, after the day of the month and year,
These words did not as well appear,
'And so long after what happened here
On the Twenty-second of July,
Thirteen-hundred and seventy-six':
And the better in memory to fix
The place of the children's last retreat,
They called it, the Pied Piper's Street –
Where any one playing on pipe or tabor
Was sure for the future to lose his labour
Nor suffered they hostelry or tavern
To shock with mirth a street so solemn;
But opposite the place of the cavern
They wrote the story on a column,
And on the great Church-Window painted
The same, to make the world acquainted

How their children were stolen away;
And there it stands to this very day.

And I must not omit to say
That in Transylvania there's a tribe
Of alien people that ascribe
The outlandish ways and dress
On which their neighbours lay such stress
To their fathers and mothers having risen
Out of some subterraneous prison
Into which they were trepanned
Long time ago in a mighty band
Out of Hamelin town in Brunswick land,
But how or why, they don't understand.

Robert Browning (1812–1889)

The Walrus and the Carpenter

The sun was shining on the sea,
Shining with all his might:
He did his very best to make
The billows smooth and bright –
And this was odd, because it was
The middle of the night.

The moon was shining sulkily,
Because she thought the sun
Had got no business to be there
After the day was done –
'It's very rude of him,' she said,
'To come and spoil the fun!'

The sea was wet as wet could be,
The sands were dry as dry.
You could not see a cloud, because
No cloud was in the sky:
No birds were flying overhead –
There were no birds to fly.

The Walrus and the Carpenter
Were walking close at hand;
They wept like anything to see
Such quantities of sand;
'If this were only cleared away,'
They said, 'it *would* be grand!'

'If seven maids with seven mops
Swept it for half a year,
Do you suppose,' the Walrus said,
'That they could get it clear?'
'I doubt it,' said the Carpenter,
And shed a bitter tear.

'O Oysters, come and walk with us!'
The Walrus did beseech.
'A pleasant walk, a pleasant talk,
Along the briny beach:
We cannot do with more than four,
To give a hand to each.'

The eldest Oyster looked at him,
But never a word he said:
The eldest Oyster winked his eye,
And shook his heavy head —
Meaning to say he did not choose
To leave the oyster-bed.

But four young Oysters hurried up,
All eager for the treat:
Their coats were brushed, their faces washed,
Their shoes were clean and neat —
And this was odd, because, you know,
They hadn't any feet.

Four other Oysters followed them,
And yet another four;
And thick and fast they came at last,
And more, and more, and more —
All hopping through the frothy waves,
And scrambling to the shore.

The Walrus and the Carpenter
Walked on a mile or so,
And then they rested on a rock
Conveniently low:
And all the little Oysters stood
And waited in a row.

'The time has come,' the Walrus said,
'To talk of many things:
Of shoes – and ships – and sealing wax –
Of cabbages – and kings –
And why the sea is boiling hot –
And whether pigs have wings.'

'But wait a bit,' the Oysters cried,
'Before we have our chat;
For some of us are out of breath,
And all of us are fat!'
'No hurry!' said the Carpenter.
They thanked him much for that.

'A loaf of bread,' the Walrus said,
'Is what we chiefly need;
Pepper and vinegar besides
Are very good indeed –
Now, if you're ready, Oysters dear,
We can begin to feed.'

'But not on us,' the Oysters cried,
Turning a little blue.
'After such kindness that would be
A dismal thing to do!'
'The night is fine,' the Walrus said,
'Do you admire the view?'

'It was so kind of you to come,
And you are very nice!'
The Carpenter said nothing but,
'Cut us another slice.
I wish you were not quite so deaf –
I've had to ask you twice!'

'It seems a shame,' the Walrus said,
'To play them such a trick.
After we've brought them out so far
And made them trot so quick!'
The Carpenter said nothing but,
'The butter's spread too thick!'

'I weep for you,' the Walrus said,
'I deeply sympathize.'
With sobs and tears he sorted out
Those of the largest size,
Holding his pocket-handkerchief
Before his streaming eyes.

'O Oysters,' said the Carpenter,
'You've had a pleasant run!
Shall we be trotting home again?'
But answer came there none –
And this was scarcely odd, because
They'd eaten every one.

Lewis Carroll (1832–1898)

Mrs Malone

Mrs Malone
Lived hard by a wood
All on her lonesome
As nobody should.
With her crust on a plate
And her pot on the coal
And none but herself
To converse with, poor soul.
In a shawl and a hood
She got sticks out-o'door,
On a bit of old sacking
She slept on the floor,
And nobody nobody
Asked how she fared
Or knew how she managed,
For nobody cared.
   Why make a pother
   About an old crone?
   What for should they bother
   With Mrs Malone?

One Monday in winter
With snow on the ground
So thick that a footstep
Fell without sound,
She heard a faint frostbitten
Peck on the pane
And went to the window
To listen again.

There sat a cock-sparrow
Bedraggled and weak,

With half-open eyelid
And ice on his beak.
She threw up the sash
And she took the bird in,
And mumbled and fumbled it
Under her chin.
  'Ye're all of a smother,
  Ye're fair overblown!
  I've room fer another,'
  Said Mrs Malone.

Come Tuesday while eating
Her dry morning slice
With the sparrow a-picking
('Ain't company nice!')
She heard on her doorpost
A curious scratch,
And there was a cat
With its claw on the latch.
It was hungry and thirsty
And thin as a lath,
It mewed and it mowed
On the slithery path.
She threw the door open
And warmed up some pap,
And huddled and cuddled it
In her old lap.
  'There, there, little brother,
  Ye poor skin-an'-bone,
  There's room fer another,'
  Said Mrs Malone.

Come Wednesday while all of them
Crouched on the mat
With a crumb for the sparrow,
A sip for the cat,
There was a wailing and whining
Outside in the wood,
And there sat a vixen
With six of her brood.
She was haggard and ragged
And worn to a shred,
And her half-dozen babies
Were only half-fed,
But Mrs Malone, crying
'My! ain't they sweet!'
Happed them and lapped them
And gave them to eat.
    'You warm yerself, mother,
    Ye're cold as a stone!
    There's room fer another,'
    Said Mrs Malone.

Come Thursday a donkey
Stepped in off the road
With sores on his withers
From bearing a load.
Come Friday when icicles
Pierced the white air
Down from the mountainside
Lumbered a bear.
For each she had something,
If little, to give –
'Lord knows, the poor critters
Must all of 'em live,'
She gave them her sacking,
Her hood and her shawl,
Her loaf and her teapot –
She gave them her all
     'What with one thing and t'other
     Me fambily's grown,
     And there's room fer another,'
     Said Mrs Malone.

Come Saturday evening
When time was to sup
Mrs Malone
Had forgot to sit up.
The cat said meeow,
And the sparrow said peep,
The vixen, she's sleeping,
The bear, let her sleep.
On the back of the donkey
They bore her away,
Through trees and up mountains
Beyond night and day,
Till come Sunday morning
They brought her in state
Through the last cloudbank
As far as the Gate.
   'Who is it,' asked Peter,
   'You have with you there?'
   And donkey and sparrow,
   Cat, vixen, and bear

Exclaimed, 'Do you tell us
Up here she's unknown?
It's our mother, God bless us!
It's Mrs Malone,
Whose havings were few
And whose holding was small
And whose heart was so big
It had room for us all.'
Then Mrs Malone
Of a sudden awoke,
She rubbed her two eyeballs
And anxiously spoke:
'Where am I, to goodness,
And what do I see?
My dear, let's turn back,
This ain't no place fer me!'
But Peter said, 'Mother
Go in to the Throne.
There's room for another
One, Mrs Malone.'

Eleanor Farjeon
(1881–1965)

Milking Song

(extract from The High Tide on the
Coast of Lincolnshire, 1571)

'Cusha! Cusha! Cusha!' calling,
'For the dews will soone be falling;
Leave your meadow grasses mellow,
   Mellow, mellow;
Quit your cowslips, cowslips yellow;
Come uppe Whitefoot, come uppe Lightfoot;
Quit the stalks of parsley hollow,
   Hollow, hollow;
Come uppe Jetty, rise and follow,
From the clovers lift your head;
Come uppe Whitefoot, come uppe Lightfoot,
Come uppe Jetty, rise and follow,
Jetty, to the milking shed.'

Jean Ingelow
(1820–1897)

Any Prince to Any Princess

August is coming
and the goose, I'm afraid,
is getting fat.
There have been
no golden eggs for some months now.
Straw has fallen well below market price
despite my frantic spinning
and the sedge is,
as you rightly point out,
withered.

I can't imagine how the pea
got under your mattress. I apologize
humbly. The chambermaid has, of course,
been sacked. As has the frog footman.
I understand that, during my recent fact-finding tour
    of the Golden River,
despite your nightly unavailing efforts,
he remained obstinately
froggish.

I hope that the Three Wishes granted by the General
    Assembly
will go some way towards redressing
this unfortunate recent sequence of events.
The fall in output from the shoe-factory, for example:
no one could have foreseen the work-to-rule
by the National Union of Elves. Not to mention
    the fact
that the court has been fast asleep
for the last six and a half years.

The matter of the poisoned apple has been taken up
by the Board of Trade: I think I can assure you
the incident will not be
repeated.

I can quite understand, in the circumstances,
your reluctance to let down
your golden tresses. However
I feel I must point out
that the weather isn't getting any better
and I already have a nasty chill
from waiting at the base
of the White Tower. You must see the absurdity of the
situation.
Some of the courtiers are beginning to talk,
not to mention the humble villagers.
It's been three weeks now, and not even
a word.

Princess,
a cold, black wind
howls through our empty palace.
Dead leaves litter the bedchamber;
the mirror on the wall hasn't said a thing
since you left. I can only ask,
bearing all this in mind,
that you think again,

let down your hair,

reconsider.

                                        Adrian Henri (1932–)

Hiawatha's Childhood

(extract from The Story of Hiawatha)

By the shores of Gitche Gumee,
By the shining Big-Sea-Water,
Stood the wigwam of Nokomis,
Daughter of the Moon, Nokomis.
Dark behind it rose the forest,
Rose the black and gloomy pine-trees,
Rose the firs with cones upon them;
Bright before it beat the water,
Beat the clear and sunny water,
Beat the shining Big-Sea-Water.
   There the wrinkled, old Nokomis
Nursed the little Hiawatha,
Rocked him in his linden cradle,
Bedded soft in moss and rushes,
Safely bound with reindeer sinews;
Stilled his fretful wail by saying,

'Hush! the Naked Bear will get thee!'
Lulled him into slumber, singing,
'Ewa-yea! my little owlet!
Who is this, that lights the wigwam?
With his great eyes lights the wigwam?
Ewa-yea! my little owlet!'
    Many things Nokomis taught him
Of the stars that shine in heaven;
Showed him Ishkoodah, the comet,
Ishkoodah, with fiery tresses;
Showed the Death-Dance of the spirits.
Warriors with their plumes and war-clubs,
Flaring far away to northward
In the frosty nights of Winter;
Showed the broad, white road in heaven,
Pathway of the ghosts, the shadows,
Running straight across the heavens,
Crowded with the ghosts, the shadows.
    At the door on Summer evenings
Sat the little Hiawatha;
Heard the whispering of the pine-trees,
Heard the lapping of the water,
Sounds of music, words of wonder;
'Minne-wawa!' said the pine-trees,
'Mudway-aushka!' said the water.
    Saw the fire-fly, Wah-wah-taysee,
Flitting through the dusk of evening,
With the twinkle of its candle
Lighting up the brakes and bushes,
And he sang the song of children,
Sang the song Nokomis taught him:

'Wah-wah-taysee, little fire-fly,
Little, flitting, white-fire insect,
Little, dancing, white-fire creature,
Light me with your little candle,
Ere upon my bed I lay me,
Ere in sleep I close my eyelids!'
　　Saw the moon rise from the water,
Rippling, rounding from the water,
Saw the flecks and shadows on it,
Whispered, 'What is that, Nokomis?'
And the good Nokomis answered:
'Once a warrior, very angry,
Seized his grandmother, and threw her
Up into the sky at midnight;
Right against the moon he threw her;
'Tis her body that you see there.'
　　Saw the rainbow in the heaven,
In the eastern sky the rainbow,
Whispered, 'What is that, Nokomis?'
And the good Nokomis answered:
''Tis the heaven of flowers you see there;
All the wild-flowers of the forest,
All the lilies of the prairie,
When on earth they fade and perish,
Blossom in that heaven above us.'
　　When he heard the owls at midnight,
Hooting, laughing in the forest,
'What is that?' he cried in terror;
'What is that,' he said, 'Nokomis?'
And the good Nokomis answered:

'That is but the owl and owlet,
Talking in their native language,
Talking, scolding at each other.'

Then the little Hiawatha
Learned of every bird its language,
Learned their names and all their secrets,
How they built their nests in Summer,
Where they hid themselves in Winter,
Talked with them whene'er he met them,
Called them 'Hiawatha's Chickens.'
   Of all beasts he learned the language,
Learned their names and all their secrets,
How the beavers built their lodges,
Where the squirrels hid their acorns,
How the reindeer ran so swiftly,
Why the rabbit was so timid,
Talked with them whene'er he met them,
Called them 'Hiawatha's Brothers.'

H. W. Longfellow (1807–1887)

Journey of the Magi

'A cold coming we had of it,
Just the worst time of the year
For a journey, and such a long journey:
The ways deep and the weather sharp,
The very dead of winter.'
And the camels galled, sore-footed, refractory,
Lying down in the melting snow.
There were times we regretted
The summer palaces on slopes, the terraces,
And the silken girls bringing sherbet.
Then the camel men cursing and grumbling
And running away, and wanting their liquor and women,
And the night-fires going out, and the lack of shelters,
And the cities hostile and the towns unfriendly
And the villages dirty and charging high prices:
A hard time we had of it.
At the end we preferred to travel all night,
Sleeping in snatches,
With the voices singing in our ears, saying
That this was all folly.

Then at dawn we came down to a temperate valley,
Wet, below the snow line, smelling of vegetation;
With a running stream and a water-mill beating the darkness,
And three trees on the low sky,
And an old white horse galloped away in the meadow.
Then we came to a tavern with vine-leaves over the lintel,
Six hands at an open door dicing for pieces of silver,
And feet kicking the empty wine-skins.
But there was no information, and so we continued
And arrived at evening, not a moment too soon
Finding the place; it was (you may say) satisfactory.

All this was a long time ago, I remember,
And I would do it again, but set down
This set down
This: were we led all that way for
Birth or Death? There was a Birth, certainly,
We had evidence and no doubt. I had seen birth and death
But had thought they were different; this Birth was
Hard and bitter agony for us, like Death, our death.
We returned to our places, these Kingdoms,
But no longer at ease here, in the old dispensation,
With an alien people clutching their gods.
I should be glad of another death.

T. S. Eliot (1888–1965)

Disobedience

James James
Morrison Morrison
Weatherby George Dupree
Took great
Care of his Mother,
Though he was only three.
James James
Said to his Mother,
'Mother,' he said, said he;
'You must never go down to the end of the
town, if you don't go down with me.'

James James
Morrison's Mother
Put on a golden gown,
James James
Morrison's Mother
Drove to the end of the town.
James James
Morrison's Mother
Said to herself, said she:
'I can get right down to the end of the town
and be back in time for tea.'

King John
Put up a notice,
'LOST or STOLEN or STRAYED!
JAMES JAMES
MORRISON'S MOTHER
SEEMS TO HAVE BEEN MISLAID.

LAST SEEN
WANDERING VAGUELY:
QUITE OF HER OWN ACCORD,
SHE TRIED TO GET DOWN TO THE
END OF THE TOWN – FORTY
SHILLINGS REWARD!'

James James
Morrison Morrison
(Commonly known as Jim)
Told his
Other relations
Not to go blaming *him*.
James James
Said to his Mother,
'Mother,' he said, said he:
'You must *never* go down to the end of
the town without consulting me.'

James James
Morrison's mother
Hasn't been heard of since.
King John
Said he was sorry,
So did the Queen and Prince.
King John
(Somebody told me)
Said to a man he knew:
'If people go down to the end of the
town, well, what can *anyone* do?'

(Now then, very softly)
    J.J.
    M. M.
    W. G. Du P.
    Took great
    C/o his M★★★★★
    Though he was only 3.
    J.J.
    Said to his M★★★★★
    'M★★★★★,' he said, said he:
'You-must-never-go-down-to-the-end-of-the-town-
    if-you-don't-go-down-with ME!'

A. A. Milne (1882–1956)

A Visit from St. Nicholas

'Twas the night before Christmas, when all through the house
Not a creature was stirring, not even a mouse;
The stockings were hung by the chimney with care,
In hopes that St. Nicholas soon would be there;
The children were nestled all snug in their beds,
While visions of sugar-plums danced in their heads;
And mamma in her 'kerchief, and I in my cap,
Had just settled our brains for a long winter's nap –
When out on the lawn there arose such a clatter,
I sprang from my bed to see what was the matter.
Away to the window I flew like a flash,
Tore open the shutters, and threw up the sash.

The moon, on the breast of the new-fallen snow,
Gave the lustre of midday to objects below;
When, what to my wondering eyes should appear,
But a miniature sleigh and eight tiny reindeer,
With a little old driver, so lively and quick,
I knew in a moment it must be St. Nick.
More rapid than eagles his coursers they came,
And he whistled, and shouted, and called them by name:
'Now, *Dasher*! now, *Dancer*! now, *Prancer* and *Vixen*!
On, *Comet*! on, *Cupid*! on, *Donner* and *Blitzen*!
To the top of the porch! to the top of the wall!
Now dash away! dash away! dash away all!'
As dry leaves that before the wild hurricane fly,
When they meet with an obstacle, mount to the sky;
So up to the house-top the coursers they flew
With the sleigh full of toys, and St. Nicholas too.
And then, in a twinkling, I heard on the roof
The prancing and pawing of each little hoof –
As I drew in my head, and was turning around,
Down the chimney St. Nicholas came with a bound.
He was dressed all in fur, from his head to his foot,
And his clothes were all tarnished with ashes and soot;
A bundle of toys he had flung on his back,
And he looked like a pedlar just opening his pack.
His eyes – how they twinkled; his dimples, how merry!
His cheeks were like roses, his nose like a cherry!
His droll little mouth was drawn up like a bow,
And the beard of his chin was as white as the snow;
The stump of a pipe he held tight in his teeth,
And the smoke it encircled his head like a wreath;

He had a broad face and a little round belly
That shook, when he laughed, like a bowl full of jelly.
He was chubby and plump, a right jolly old elf,
And I laughed when I saw him, in spite of myself;
A wink of his eye and a twist of his head
Soon gave me to know I had nothing to dread;
He spoke not a word, but went straight to his work,
And filled all the stockings; then turned with a jerk,
And laying his finger aside of his nose,
And giving a nod, up the chimney he rose;
He sprang to his sleigh, to his team gave a whistle,
And away they all flew like the down of a thistle.
But I heard him exclaim, ere he drove out of sight,
'*Happy Christmas to all, and to all a good night!*'

Clement Clarke Moore (1779–1863)

Lucy Gray; or, Solitude

Oft I had heard of Lucy Gray:
And, when I crossed the wild,
I chanced to see at break of day
The solitary child.

No mate, no comrade Lucy knew;
She dwelt on a wide moor,
– The sweetest thing that ever grew
Beside a human door!

You yet may spy the fawn at play,
The hare upon the green;
But the sweet face of Lucy Gray
Will never more be seen.

'To-night will be a stormy night –
You to the town must go;
And take a lantern, Child, to light
Your mother through the snow.'

'That, Father! will I gladly do:
'Tis scarcely afternoon –
The minster-clock has just struck two,
And yonder is the moon!'

At this the Father raised his hook,
And snapped a faggot-band;
He plied his work; – and Lucy took
The lantern in her hand.

Not blither is the mountain roe:
With many a wanton stroke
Her feet disperse the powdery snow,
That rises up like smoke.

The storm came on before its time:
She wandered up and down;
And many a hill did Lucy climb:
But never reached the town.

The wretched parents all that night
Went shouting far and wide;
But there was neither sound nor sight
To serve them for a guide.

At day-break on a hill they stood
They overlooked the moor;
And thence they saw the bridge of wood,
A furlong from their door.

They wept – and, turning homeward, cried,
'In heaven we all shall meet;'
– When in the snow the mother spied
The print of Lucy's feet.

Then downwards from the steep hill's edge
They tracked the footmarks small;
And through the broken hawthorn hedge,
And by the long stone-wall;

And then an open field they crossed:
The marks were still the same;
They tracked them on, nor ever lost;
And to the bridge they came.

They followed from the snowy bank
Those footmarks, one by one,
Into the middle of the plank;
And further there were none!

−Yet some maintain that to this day
She is a living child;
That you may see sweet Lucy Gray
Upon the lonesome wild.

O'er rough and smooth she trips along,
And never looks behind;
And sings a solitary song
That whistles in the wind.

William Wordsworth (1770–1850)

Macavity: the Mystery Cat

Macavity's a Mystery Cat: he's called the Hidden Paw −
For he's the master criminal who can defy the Law.
He's the bafflement of Scotland Yard, the Flying Squad's despair:
For when they reach the scene of crime − *Macavity's not there!*

Macavity, Macavity, there's no one like Macavity,
He's broken every human law, he breaks the law of gravity.
His powers of levitation would make a fakir stare,
And when you reach the scene of crime − Macavity's not there!
You may seek him in the basement, you may look up in the air −
But I tell you once and once again − *Macavity's not there!*

Macavity's a ginger cat, he's very tall and thin;
You would know him if you saw him, for his eyes are sunken in.
His brow is deeply lined with thought, his head is highly domed;
His coat is dusty from neglect, his whiskers are uncombed.
He sways his head from side to side, with movements like a snake;
And when you think he's half asleep, he's always wide awake.

Macavity, Macavity, there's no one like Macavity,
For he's a fiend in feline shape, a monster of depravity.
You may meet him in a by-street, you may see him in the square –
But when a crime's discovered, then *Macavity's not there*!

He's outwardly respectable. (They say he cheats at cards.)
And his footprints are not found in any file of Scotland Yard's.
And when the larder's looted, or the jewel-case is rifled,
Or when the milk is missing, or another Peke's been stifled,
Or the greenhouse glass is broken, and the trellis past repair –
Ay, there's the wonder of the thing! *Macavity's not there*!

And when the Foreign Office find a Treaty's gone astray,
Or the Admiralty lose some plans and drawings by the way,
There may be a scrap of paper in the hall or on the stair –
But it's useless to investigate – *Macavity's not there*!
And when the loss has been disclosed, the Secret Service say:
'It *must* have been Macavity!' – but he's a mile away.
You'll be sure to find him resting, or a-licking of his thumbs,
Or engaged in doing complicated long division sums.

Macavity, Macavity, there's no one like Macavity,
There never was a Cat of such deceitfulness and suavity.
He always has an alibi, and one or two to spare:
At whatever time the deed took place – MACAVITY WASN'T THERE!
And they say that all the Cats whose wicked deeds are widely known
(I might mention Mungojerrie, I might mention Griddlebone)
Are nothing more than agents for the Cat who all the time
Just controls their operations: the Napoleon of Crime!

T. S. Eliot (1888–1965)

HOPES &
DREAMS

'Oh, to be an eagle'

Home Thoughts from Abroad

Oh, to be in England
Now that April's there,
And whoever wakes in England
Sees, some morning, unaware,
That the lowest boughs and the brushwood sheaf
Round the elm-tree bole are in tiny leaf,
While the chaffinch sings on the orchard bough
In England – now!
And after April, when May follows,
And the whitethroat builds, and all the swallows!
Hark, where my blossomed pear-tree in the hedge
Leans to the field and scatters on the clover
Blossoms and dewdrops – at the bent spray's edge –
That's the wise thrush; he sings each song twice over,
Lest you should think he never could recapture
The first fine careless rapture!
And though the fields look rough with hoary dew,
All will be gay when noontide wakes anew
The buttercups, the little children's dower
– Far brighter than this gaudy melon-flower.

Robert Browning (1812–1889)

A Small Dragon

I've found a small dragon in the woodshed.
Think it must have come from deep inside a forest
because it's damp and green and leaves
are still reflecting in its eyes.

I fed it on many things, tried grass,
the roots of stars, hazel-nut and dandelion,
but it stared up at me as if to say, I need
foods you can't provide.

It made a nest among the coal,
not unlike a bird's but larger,
it is out of place here
and is quite silent.

If you believed in it I would come
hurrying to your house to let you share my wonder,
but I want instead to see
if you yourself will pass this way.

Brian Patten (1946–)

Up-hill

Does the road wind up-hill all the way?
　　Yes, to the very end.
Will the day's journey take the whole long day?
　　From morn to night, my friend.

But is there for the night a resting-place?
　　A roof for when the slow dark hours begin.
May not the darkness hide it from my face?
　　You cannot miss that inn.

Shall I meet other wayfarers at night?
　　Those who have gone before.
Then must I knock, or call when just in sight?
　　They will not keep you standing at that door.

Shall I find comfort, travel-sore and weak?
　　Of labour you shall find the sum.
Will there be beds for me and all who seek?
　　Yea, beds for all who come.

Christina Rossetti (1830–1895)

If—

If you can keep your head when all about you
Are losing theirs and blaming it on you,
If you can trust yourself when all men doubt you,
But make allowance for their doubting too;
If you can wait and not be tired of waiting,
Or being lied about, don't deal in lies,
Or being hated, don't give way to hating,
And yet don't look too good, nor talk too wise:

If you can dream – and not make dreams your master;
If you can think – and not make thoughts your aim;
If you can meet with Triumph and Disaster
And treat those two impostors just the same;
If you can bear to hear the truth you've spoken
Twisted by knaves to make a trap for fools,
Or watch the things you gave your life to, broken,
And stoop and build 'em up with worn-out tools:

If you can make one heap of all your winnings
And risk it on one turn of pitch-and-toss,
And lose, and start again at your beginnings
And never breathe a word about your loss;
If you can force your heart and nerve and sinew
To serve your turn long after they are gone,
And so hold on when there is nothing in you
Except the Will which says to them: 'Hold on!'

If you can talk with crowds and keep your virtue,
Or walk with Kings – nor lose the common touch,
If neither foes nor loving friends can hurt you,
If all men count with you, but none too much;
If you can fill the unforgiving minute
With sixty seconds' worth of distance run,
Yours is the Earth and everything that's in it,
And – which is more – you'll be a Man, my son!

Rudyard Kipling (1865–1936)

Warning

When I am an old woman I shall wear purple
With a red hat which doesn't suit me,
And I shall spend my pension on brandy and
   summer gloves
And satin sandals, and say we've no money for butter.
I shall sit down on the pavement when I'm tired
And gobble up samples in shops and press alarm bells
And run my stick along the public railings
And make up for the sobriety of my youth.
I shall go out in my slippers in the rain
And pick the flowers in other people's gardens
And learn to spit.

You can wear terrible shirts and grow more fat
And eat three pounds of sausages at a go
Or only bread and pickle for a week
And hoard pens and pencils and beermats and things
   in boxes.

But now we must have clothes that keep us dry
And pay the rent and not swear in the street
And set a good example for the children.
We must have friends to dinner and read the papers.

But maybe I ought to practise a little now?
So people who know me are not too shocked
   and surprised
When suddenly I am old and start to wear purple.

Jenny Joseph (1932–)

Wishes of an Elderly Man

I wish I loved the Human Race;
I wish I loved its silly face;
I wish I liked the way it walks;
I wish I liked the way it talks;
And when I'm introduced to one
I wish I thought *What Jolly Fun!*

Sir Walter Raleigh (1552–1618)

You Can't Be That

I told them:
When I grow up
I'm not going to be a scientist
Or someone who reads the news on TV.
No, a million birds will fly through me.
I'M GOING TO BE A TREE!

They said,
You can't be that. No, you can't be that.

I told them:
When I grow up
I'm not going to be an airline pilot,
A dancer, a lawyer or an MC.
No, huge whales will swim in me.
I'M GOING TO BE AN OCEAN!

They said,
You can't be that. No, you can't be that.

I told them:
I'm not going to be a DJ,
A computer programmer, a musician or beautician.
No, streams will flow through me,
I'll be the home of eagles;
I'll be full of nooks, crannies, valleys and fountains.
I'M GOING TO BE A RANGE OF
MOUNTAINS!

They said,
You can't be that. No, you can't be that.

I asked them:
Just what do you think I am?
Just a child, they said,
And children always become
At least one of the things
We want them to be.

They do not understand me.
I'll be a stable if I want, smelling of fresh hay,
I'll be a lost glade in which unicorns still play.
They do not realize I can fulfil any ambition.
They do not realize among them
Walks a magician.

Brian Patten (1946–)

Aedh Wishes for the Cloths of Heaven

Had I the heavens' embroider'd cloths,
Enwrought with golden and silver light,
The blue and the dim and the dark cloths
Of night and light and the half light;
I would spread the cloths under your feet:
But I, being poor, have only my dreams;
I have spread my dreams under your feet;
Tread softly because you tread on my dreams.

W. B. Yeats (1865–1939)

Piano

Softly, in the dusk, a woman is singing to me;
Taking me back down the vista of years, till I see
A child sitting under the piano, in the boom of the tingling strings
And pressing the small, poised feet of a mother who smiles as she sings.

In spite of myself, the insidious mastery of song
Betrays me back, till the heart of me weeps to belong
To the old Sunday evenings at home, with winter outside
And hymns in the cosy parlour, the tinkling piano our guide.

So now it is vain for the singer to burst into clamour
With the great black piano appassionato. The glamour
Of childish days is upon me, my manhood is cast
Down in the flood of remembrance, I weep like a child for the past.

D. H. Lawrence (1885–1930)

Ode to a Nightingale

My heart aches, and a drowsy numbness pains
    My sense, as though of hemlock I had drunk,
Or emptied some dull opiate to the drains
    One minute past, and Lethe-wards had sunk:
'Tis not through envy of thy happy lot,
    But being too happy in thy happiness, –
        That thou, light-winged Dryad of the trees,
            In some melodious plot
Of beechen green, and shadows numberless,
    Singest of summer in full-throated ease.

O, for a draught of vintage! that hath been
   Cool'd a long age in the deep-delved earth,
Tasting of Flora and the country green,
   Dance, and Provençal song, and sunburnt mirth!
O, for a beaker full of the warm South,
   Full of the true, the blushful Hippocrene,
     With beaded bubbles winking at the brim,
       And purple-stained mouth;
   That I might drink, and leave the world unseen,
    And with thee fade away into the forest dim:

Fade far away, dissolve, and quite forget
   What thou among the leaves hast never known,
The weariness, the fever, and the fret
   Here, where men sit and hear each other groan;
Where palsy shakes a few, sad, last gray hairs,
   Where youth grows pale, and spectre-thin, and dies;
    Where but to think is to be full of sorrow
      And leaden-eyed despairs;
   Where Beauty cannot keep her lustrous eyes,
    Or new Love pine at them beyond to-morrow.

Away! away! for I will fly to thee,
   Not charioted by Bacchus and his pards,
But on the viewless wings of Poesy,
   Though the dull brain perplexes and retards:
Already with thee! tender is the night,
   And haply the Queen-Moon is on her throne,
     Cluster'd around by all her starry Fays;
       But here there is no light,
Save what from heaven is with the breezes blown
   Through verdurous glooms and winding mossy ways.

I cannot see what flowers are at my feet,
   Nor what soft incense hangs upon the boughs,
But, in embalmed darkness, guess each sweet
   Wherewith the seasonable month endows
The grass, the thicket, and the fruit-tree wild;
   White hawthorn, and the pastoral eglantine;
     Fast fading violets cover'd up in leaves;
       And mid-May's eldest child,
The coming musk-rose, full of dewy wine,
   The murmurous haunt of flies on summer eves.

Darkling I listen; and for many a time
   I have been half in love with easeful Death,
Call'd him soft names in many a mused rhyme,
   To take into the air my quiet breath;
Now more than ever seems it rich to die,
   To cease upon the midnight with no pain,
     While thou art pouring forth thy soul abroad
       In such an ecstasy!
Still wouldst thou sing, and I have ears in vain —
   To thy high requiem become a sod.

Thou wast not born for death, immortal Bird!
  No hungry generations tread thee down;
The voice I hear this passing night was heard
  In ancient days by emperor and clown:
Perhaps the self-same song that found a path
  Through the sad heart of Ruth, when, sick for home,
    She stood in tears amid the alien corn;
        The same that oft-times hath
  Charm'd magic casements, opening on the foam
  Of perilous seas, in faery lands forlorn.

Forlorn! the very word is like a bell
  To toll me back from thee to my sole self!
Adieu! the fancy cannot cheat so well
  As she is fam'd to do, deceiving elf.
Adieu! adieu! thy plaintive anthem fades
  Past the near meadows, over the still stream,
    Up the hill-side; and now 'tis buried deep
        In the next valley-glades:
  Was it a vision, or a waking dream?
  Fled is that music: – Do I wake or sleep?

John Keats (1795–1821)

My Heart's in the Highlands

My heart's in the Highlands, my heart is not here;
My heart's in the Highlands a-chasing the deer;
Chasing the wild deer, and following the roe,
My heart's in the Highlands wherever I go.
Farewell to the Highlands, farewell to the North,
The birth-place of valour, the country of worth;
Wherever I wander, wherever I rove,
The hills of the Highlands for ever I love.

Farewell to the mountains, high covered with snow;
Farewell to the straths and green valleys below;
Farewell to the forests and wild-hanging woods;
Farewell to the torrents and loud-pouring floods.
My heart's in the Highlands, my heart is not here;
My heart's in the Highlands a-chasing the deer;
Chasing the wild deer, and following the roe,
My heart's in the Highlands, wherever I go.

Robert Burns (1759–1796)

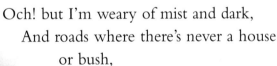
An Old Woman of the Roads

O, to have a little house!
To own the hearth and stool and all!
The heaped-up sods upon the fire,
The pile of turf against the wall!

To have a clock with weights and chains
And pendulum swinging up and down,
A dresser filled with shining delph,
Speckled and white and blue and brown!

I could be busy all the day
Clearing and sweeping hearth and floor,
And fixing on their shelf again
My white and blue and speckled store!

I could be quiet there at night
Beside the fire and by myself,
Sure of a bed and loth to leave
The ticking clock and shining delph!

Och! but I'm weary of mist and dark,
And roads where there's never a house
or bush,
And tired I am of bog and road,
And the crying wind and the
lonesome hush!

And I am praying to God on high,
And I am praying Him night and day,
For a little house, a house of my own –
Out of the wind's and the rain's way.

Padraic Colum (1881–1972)

The Garden's Full of Witches

Mum! The garden's full of witches!
Come quick and see the witches.
    There's a full moon out,
    And they're flying about,
Come on! You'll miss the witches.

Oh Mum! You're missing the witches.
You have never seen so many witches.
    They are casting spells!
    There are horrible smells!
Come on! You'll miss the witches.

Mum, hurry! Come look at the witches.
The shrubbery's bursting with witches.
  They've turned our Joan
  Into a garden gnome.
Come on! You'll miss the witches.

Oh no! You'll miss the witches.
The garden's black with witches.
  Come on! Come on!
  Too late! They've gone.
Oh, you always miss the witches!

Colin McNaughton (1951–)

Two Men Looked Out

Two men looked out through prison bars;
The one saw mud, the other stars.

Anon.

Tarantella

Do you remember an Inn,
Miranda?
Do you remember an Inn?
And the tedding and the spreading
Of the straw for a bedding,
And the fleas that tease in the High Pyrenees,
And the wine that tasted of the tar?
And the cheers and the jeers of the young muleteers
(Under the vine of the dark verandah)?
Do you remember an Inn, Miranda,
Do you remember an Inn?
And the cheers and the jeers of the young muleteers
Who hadn't got a penny,
And who weren't paying any,
And the hammer at the doors and the Din?
And the Hip! Hop! Hap!
Of the clap
Of the hands to the twirl and the swirl
Of the girl gone chancing,
Glancing,
Dancing,
Backing and advancing,
Snapping of a clapper to the spin
Out and in –
And the Ting, Tong, Tang of the Guitar!
Do you remember an Inn,
Miranda?
Do you remember an Inn?

Never more;
Miranda,
Never more.
Only the high peaks hoar:
And Aragon a torrent at the door.
No sound
In the walls of the Halls where falls
The tread
Of the feet of the dead to the ground
No sound:
But the boom
Of the far Waterfall like Doom.

Hilaire Belloc (1870–1953)

'O tan-faced prairie-boy'

O tan-faced prairie-boy,
Before you came to camp came many a welcome gift,
Praises and presents came and nourishing food,
   till at last among the recruits,
You came, taciturn, with nothing to give – we but
   look'd on each other,
When lo! more than all the gifts of the world you gave me.

Walt Whitman (1819–1892)

Oh, To Be . . .

'Oh, to be an eagle
And to swoop down from a peak
With the golden sunlight flashing
From the fierce hook of my beak.

'Oh, to be an eagle
And to terrify the sky
With a beat of wings like thunder
And a wild, barbaric cry.

'Oh . . . but why keep dreaming?
I must learn to be myself,'
Said the rubber duckling sadly
On its soapy bathroom shelf.

Richard Edwards (1949–)

Stuff & Nonsense

'Sssnnnwhuffffll?'

You are Old, Father William

'You are old, Father William,' the young man said,
'And your hair has become very white;
And yet you incessantly stand on your head –
Do you think, at your age, it is right?'

'In my youth,' Father William replied to his son,
'I feared it might injure the brain;
But, now that I'm perfectly sure I have none,
Why, I do it again and again.'

'You are old,' said the youth, 'as I mentioned before,
And have grown most uncommonly fat;
Yet you turned a back-somersault in at the door –
Pray, what is the reason of that?'

'In my youth,' said the sage, as he shook his grey locks,
'I kept all my limbs very supple
By the use of this ointment – one shilling the box –
Allow me to sell you a couple?'

'You are old,' said the youth, 'and your jaws are too weak
For anything tougher than suet;
Yet you finished the goose, with the bones and the beak –
Pray, how did you manage to do it?'

'In my youth,' said his father, 'I took to the law,
And argued each case with my wife;
And the muscular strength, which it gave to my jaw,
Has lasted the rest of my life.'

'You are old,' said the youth, 'one would hardly suppose
That your eye was as steady as ever;
Yet you balanced an eel on the end of your nose –
What made you so awfully clever?'

'I have answered three questions, and that is enough,'
Said his father. 'Don't give yourself airs!
Do you think I can listen all day to such stuff?
Be off, or I'll kick you downstairs!'

Lewis Carroll (1832–1898)

Lines on Montezuma

Mexican legend by a Passman

Montezuma
Met a puma
Coming through the rye:
Montezuma made the puma
Into apple pie.

Invitation
To the nation
Everyone to come.
Montezuma
And the puma
Give a kettle-drum.

Acceptation
Of the nation
One and all invited.
Montezuma
And the puma
Equally delighted.

Preparation,
Ostentation,
Dresses rich prepared:
Feathers – jewels –
Work in crewels –
No expenses spared.

Congregation
Of the nation
Round the palace wall.
Awful rumour
That the puma
Won't be served to all.

Deputation
From the nation,
Audience they gain.
'What's this rumour?
Montezuma,
If you please, explain.'

Montezuma
(Playful humour
very well sustained)
Answers: 'Piedish
As it's my dish,
Is for me retained.'

Exclamation!
Indignation!
Feeling running high.
Montezuma
Joins the puma
In the apple pie.

D. F. Alderson

Names of Scottish Islands to be Shouted in a Bus Queue When You're Feeling Bored

Yell!

Muck!

Eigg!

Rum!

Uist!

Hoy!

Foula!

Coll!

Canna!

Barra!

Gigha!

Jura!

Pabay!

Raasay!

Skye!

Ian McMillan (1956–)

Humpty Dumpty's Recitation

In winter, when the fields are white,
I sing this song for your delight –

In spring, when woods are getting green,
I'll try and tell you what I mean.

In summer, when the days are long,
Perhaps you'll understand the song.

In autumn, when the leaves are brown,
Take pen and ink and write it down.

I sent a message to the fish:
I told them 'This is what I wish.'

The little fishes of the sea
They sent an answer back to me.

The little fishes' answer was
'We cannot do it, Sir, because –'

I sent to them again to say
'It will be better to obey.'

The fishes answered with a grin,
'Why, what a temper you are in!'

I told them once, I told them twice:
They would not listen to advice.

I took a kettle large and new,
Fit for the deed I had to do.

My heart went hop, my heart went thump;
I filled the kettle at the pump.

Then someone came to me and said
'The little fishes are in bed.'

I said to him, I said it plain,
'Then you must wake them up again.'

I said it loud and very clear;
I went and shouted in his ear.

But he was very stiff and proud;
He said 'You needn't shout so loud!'

And he was very proud and stiff;
He said 'I'll go and wake them, if —'

I took a corkscrew from the shelf:
I went to wake them up myself.

And when I found the door was locked,
I pulled and pushed and kicked and knocked.

And when I found the door was shut,
I tried to turn the handle, but —

Lewis Carroll (1832–1898)

'O, know you the land'

O, know you the land where the cheese-tree grows,
And the unicorn spins on the end of his nose;
Where the sea-mew scowls on the circling bat,
And the elephant hunts in an opera hat?

'Tis there that I lie with my head in a pond,
And play with a valueless Tichborne bond;
'Tis there that I sip pure Horniman's tea
To the sound of the gong and the howling sea.

'Tis there that I revel in soapsuds and rum,
And wait till my creditors choose to come;
'Tis there that I dream of the days when I
Shall soar to the moon through the red-hot sky.

Then come, oh come to that happy land!
And don't forget your galvanic band;
We will play at cards in the lion's den,
And go to bed when the clock strikes ten.

Anon.

The Bubble

I blew myself a bubble
That was bigger than myself
And I floated up inside it
To the top-most shelf,

And there I saw before me
With my own two eyes
Half a hundred jam-pots
And four dead flies.

I blew myself a bubble
That was larger than Papa
And he floated off inside it
To a place afar,

As everybody cheered and waved
To see him overhead
'Your Father is a very clever man,'
They said.

Kenneth Hopkins (1914–)

What a Wonderful Bird the Frog Are

What a wonderful bird the frog are: –
When he sit, he stand almost:
When he hop, he fly almost.
He ain't got no sense hardly:
He ain't got no tail either.
When he sit, he sit on what he ain't got – almost.

Anon.

The Jumblies

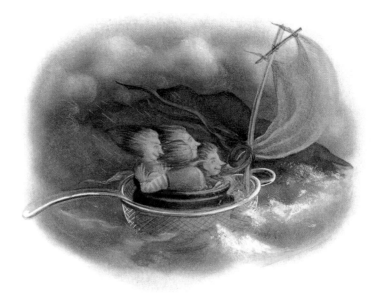

They went to sea in a Sieve, they did,
    In a Sieve they went to sea:
In spite of all their friends could say,
On a winter's morn, on a stormy day,
    In a Sieve they went to sea!
And when the Sieve turned round and round,
And every one cried, 'You'll all be drowned!'
They called aloud, 'Our Sieve ain't big,
But we don't care a button! we don't care a fig!
    In a Sieve we'll go to sea!'
        Far and few, far and few,
            Are the lands where the Jumblies live;
            Their heads are green, and their hands are blue,
                And they went to sea in a Sieve.

They sailed away in a Sieve, they did,
  In a Sieve they sailed so fast,
With only a beautiful pea-green veil
Tied with a riband by way of a sail,
  To a small tobacco-pipe mast;
And every one said, who saw them go,
'O won't they be soon upset, you know!
For the sky is dark, and the voyage is long,
And happen what may, it's extremely wrong
  In a Sieve to sail so fast!'
    Far and few, far and few,
      Are the lands where the Jumblies live;
      Their heads are green, and their hands are blue,
      And they went to sea in a Sieve.

The water it soon came in, it did,
  The water it soon came in;
So to keep them dry, they wrapped their feet
In a pinky paper all folded neat,
  And they fastened it down with a pin.
And they passed the night in a crockery-jar,
And each of them said, 'How wise we are!
Though the sky be dark, and the voyage be long,
Yet we never can think we were rash or wrong,
  While round in our Sieve we spin!'
    Far and few, far and few,
      Are the lands where the Jumblies live;
      Their heads are green, and their hands are blue,
      And they went to sea in a Sieve.

And all night long they sailed away;
  And when the sun went down,
They whistled and warbled a moony song
To the echoing sound of a coppery gong,
  In the shade of the mountains brown.
'O Timballo! How happy we are,
When we live in a sieve and a crockery-jar,
And all night long in the moonlight pale,
We sail away with a pea-green sail,
  In the shade of the mountains brown!'
    Far and few, far and few,
      Are the lands where the Jumblies live;
      Their heads are green, and their hands are blue,
      And they went to sea in a Sieve.

They sailed to the Western Sea, they did,
  To a land all covered with trees,
And they bought an Owl, and a useful Cart,
And a pound of Rice, and a Cranberry Tart,
  And a hive of silvery Bees.
And they bought a Pig, and some green Jack-daws,
And a lovely Monkey with lollipop paws,
And forty bottles of Ring-Bo-Ree,
  And no end of Stilton Cheese.
    Far and few, far and few,
      Are the lands where the Jumblies live;
      Their heads are green, and their hands are blue,
      And they went to sea in a Sieve.

And in twenty years they all came back,
   In twenty years or more,
And every one said, 'How tall they've grown!
For they've been to the Lakes, and the Torrible Zone,
   And the hills of the Chankly Bore;
And they drank their health, and gave them a feast
Of dumplings made of beautiful yeast;
And every one said, 'If we only live,
We too will go to sea in a Sieve, –
   To the hills of the Chankly Bore!'
      Far and few, far and few,
         Are the lands where the Jumblies live;
         Their heads are green, and their hands are blue,
            And they went to sea in a Sieve.

Edward Lear (1812–1888)

There was a Naughty Boy

There was a naughty boy,
  A naughty boy was he,
He would not stop at home,
  He could not quiet be –
    He took
    In his knapsack
    A book
    Full of vowels
    And a shirt
    With some towels,
    A slight cap
    For night cap,
    A hair brush,
    Comb ditto,
    New stockings –
    For old ones
    Would split O!
    This knapsack
    Tight at 's back
    He rivetted close
And followed his nose
  To the North,
  To the North,
And followed his nose
  To the North.

There was a naughty boy,
  And a naughty boy was he,
He ran away to Scotland
  The people for to see –
    There he found
    That the ground
    Was as hard,
    That a yard
    Was as long,
    That a song
    Was as merry,
    That a cherry
    Was as red –
    That lead
    Was as weighty
    That fourscore
    Was as eighty,
    That a door
    Was as wooden
    As in England –
So he stood in his shoes
  And he wondered,
  He wondered,
He stood in his shoes
  And he wondered.

John Keats (1795–1821)

The Loch Ness Monster's Song

Sssnnnwhuffffll?

Hnwhuffl hhnnwfl hnfl hfl?

Gdroblboblhobngbl gbl gl g g g g glbgl.

Drublhaflablhaflubhafgabhaflhafl fl fl –

gm grawwwww grf grawf awfgm graw gm.

Hovoplodok-doplodovok-plovodokot-doplodokosh?

Splgraw fok fok splgrafhatchgabrlgabrl fok splfok!

Zgra kra gka fok!

Grof grawff gahf?

Gombl mbl bl –

blm plm,

blm plm,

blm plm,

blp.

Edwin Morgan (1920–)

Mr Nobody

I know a funny little man,
As quiet as a mouse.
He does the mischief that is done
In everybody's house.
Though no one ever sees his face,
Yet one and all agree
That every plate we break, was cracked
By Mr Nobody.

'Tis he who always tears our books,
Who leaves the door ajar.
He picks the buttons from our shirts,
And scatters pins afar.
That squeaking door will always squeak –
For prithee, don't you see?
We leave the oiling to be done
By Mr Nobody.

He puts damp wood upon the fire,
That kettles will not boil:
His are the feet that bring in mud
And all the carpets soil.
The papers that so oft are lost –
Who had them last but he?
There's no one tosses them about
But Mr Nobody.

The fingermarks upon the door
By none of us were made.
We never leave the blinds unclosed
To let the curtains fade.
The ink we never spill! The boots
That lying round you see,
Are not our boots – they all belong
To Mr Nobody.

Anon.

The Little Man

As I was walking up the stair
I met a man who wasn't there;
He wasn't there again today.
I wish, I wish he'd stay away.

Hughes Mearns (1875–1965)

The Pobble Who Has No Toes

The Pobble who has no toes
    Had once as many as we;
When they said, 'Some day you may lose them all;' –
    He replied, – 'Fish fiddle de-dee!'
And his Aunt Jobiska made him drink,
Lavender water tinged with pink,
For she said, 'The World in general knows
There's nothing so good for a Pobble's toes!'

The Pobble who has no toes,
    Swam across the Bristol Channel;
But before he set out he wrapped his nose,
    In a piece of scarlet flannel.
For his Aunt Jobiska said, 'No harm
Can come to his toes if his nose is warm;
And it's perfectly known that a Pobble's toes
Are safe, – provided he minds his nose.'

The Pobble swam fast and well
  And when boats or ships came near him
He tinkledy-binkledy-winkled a bell
  So that all the world could hear him.
And all the Sailors and Admirals cried,
When they saw him nearing the further side, –
'He has gone to fish, for his Aunt Jobiska's
Runcible Cat with crimson whiskers!'

But before he touched the shore,
  The shore of the Bristol Channel,
A sea-green Porpoise carried away
  His wrapper of scarlet flannel.
And when he came to observe his feet
Formerly garnished with toes so neat
His face at once became forlorn
On perceiving that all his toes were gone!

And nobody ever knew
  From that dark day to the present,
Whoso had taken the Pobble's toes,
  In a manner so far from pleasant.
Whether the shrimps or crawfish gray,
Or crafty Mermaids stole them away –
Nobody knew; and nobody knows
How the Pobble was robbed of his twice five toes!

The Pobble who has no toes
  Was placed in a friendly Bark,
And they rowed him back, and carried him up,
  To his Aunt Jobiska's Park.
And she made him a feast at his earnest wish
Of eggs and buttercups fried with fish; –
And she said, – 'It's a fact the whole world knows,
That Pobbles are happier without their toes.'

Edward Lear (1812–1888)

RIVER & SEA

*'The tide in the river
runs deep'*

Sailing

Consider the Viking keel
Cutting keen,
Slicing over the green deep.

Hear the hiss of the salt foam
Curling off at the bow,
And the wake closing quietly
In bubbles behind.

Listen to the sound of the
    thumping drum,
See the helmets shine in the sun.
Feel, with your finger,
The full sail drawn tight
As they drive home before
    the wind.

David English (1945–)

Ariel's Song

(extract from The Tempest)

Full fathom five thy father lies;
   Of his bones are coral made:
Those are pearls that were his eyes:
   Nothing of him that doth fade,
But doth suffer a sea-change
Into something rich and strange.
Sea-nymphs hourly ring his knell:
             ding-dong.
Hark! now I hear them, – ding-dong, bell.

William Shakespeare (1564–1616)

maggie and milly and molly and may

maggie and milly and molly and may
went down to the beach(to play one day)

and maggie discovered a shell that sang
so sweetly she couldn't remember her troubles,and

milly befriended a stranded star
whose rays five languid fingers were;

and molly was chased by a horrible thing
which raced sideways while blowing bubbles:and

may came home with a smooth round stone
as small as a world and as large as alone.

For whatever we lose(like a you or a me)
it's always ourselves we find in the sea

E. E. Cummings (1894–1962)

The Rime of the Ancient Mariner
(extract)

It is an ancient Mariner,
And he stoppeth one of three.
'By thy long grey beard and glittering eye,
Now wherefore stopp'st thou me?

'The Bridegroom's doors are opened wide,
And I am next of kin;
The guests are met, the feast is set:
May'st hear the merry din.'

He holds him with his skinny hand,
'There was a ship,' quoth he.
'Hold off! unhand me, grey-beard loon!'
Eftsoons his hand dropt he.

He holds him with his glittering eye –
The Wedding-Guest stood still,
And listens like a three years' child:
The Mariner hath his will.

The Wedding-Guest sat on a stone:
He cannot choose but hear;
And thus spake on that ancient man,
The bright-eyed Mariner.

'The ship was cheer'd, the harbour clear'd,
Merrily did we drop
Below the kirk, below the hill,
Below the lighthouse top.

'The Sun came up upon the left,
Out of the sea came he!
And he shone bright, and on the right
Went down into the sea.

'Higher and higher every day,
Till over the mast at noon —'
The Wedding-Guest here beat his breast,
For he heard the loud bassoon.

The bride hath paced into the hall,
Red as a rose is she;
Nodding their heads before her goes
The merry minstrelsy.

The Wedding-Guest he beat his breast,
Yet he cannot choose but hear;
And thus spake on that ancient man,
The bright-eyed Mariner.

'And now the Storm-blast came, and he
Was tyrannous and strong:
He struck with his o'ertaking wings,
And chased us south along.

'With sloping masts and dipping prow,
As who pursued with yell and blow
Still treads the shadow of his foe,
And forward bends his head,
The ship drove fast, loud roar'd the blast,
And southward aye we fled.

'And now there came both mist and snow,
And it grew wondrous cold:
And ice, mast-high, came floating by,
As green as emerald.

'And through the drifts the snowy clifts
Did send a dismal sheen:
Nor shapes of men nor beasts we ken –
The ice was all between.

'The ice was here, the ice was there,
The ice was all around:
It crack'd and growl'd, and roar'd and howl'd,
Like noises in a swound!

'At length did cross an Albatross,
Through the fog it came;
As if it had been a Christian soul,
We hail'd it in God's name.

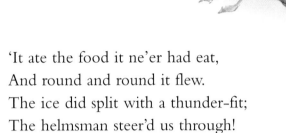

'It ate the food it ne'er had eat,
And round and round it flew.
The ice did split with a thunder-fit;
The helmsman steer'd us through!

'And a good south wind sprung up behind;
The Albatross did follow,
And every day, for food or play,
Came to the mariners' hollo!

'In mist or cloud, on mast or shroud,
It perched for vespers nine;
Whiles all the night, through fog-smoke white,
Glimmered the white Moon-shine.'

'God save thee, ancient Mariner,
From the fiends, that plague thee thus! –
Why look'st thou so?' – 'With my cross-bow
I shot the Albatross.

'The Sun now rose upon the right:
Out of the sea came he,
Still hid in mist, and on the left
Went down into the sea.

'And the good south wind still blew behind,
But no sweet bird did follow,
Nor any day for food or play
Came to the mariners' hollo!

'And I had done a hellish thing,
And it would work 'em woe:
For all averred I had killed the bird
That made the breeze to blow.
Ah wretch! said they, the bird to slay,
That made the breeze to blow!

'Nor dim nor red, like God's own head,
The glorious Sun uprist:
Then all averred I had killed the bird
That brought the fog and mist.
'Twas right, said they, such birds to slay,
That bring the fog and mist.

'The fair breeze blew, the white foam flew,
The furrow follow'd free;
We were the first that ever burst
Into that silent sea.

'Down dropt the breeze, the sails dropt down,
'Twas sad as sad could be;
And we did speak only to break
The silence of the sea!

'All in a hot and copper sky,
The bloody Sun, at noon,
Right up above the mast did stand,
No bigger than the Moon.

'Day after day, day after day,
We stuck, nor breath nor motion;
As idle as a painted ship
Upon a painted ocean.

'Water, water, every where,
And all the boards did shrink:
Water, water, every where
Nor any drop to drink.
'The very deep did rot: O Christ!
That ever this should be!
Yea, slimy things did crawl with legs
Upon the slimy sea.

'About, about, in reel and rout
The death-fires danced at night;
The water, like a witch's oils,
Burnt green, and blue, and white.

'And some in dreams assurèd were
Of the Spirit that plagued us so;
Nine fathom deep he had follow'd us
From the land of mist and snow.

'And every tongue, through utter drought,
Was wither'd at the root;
We could not speak, no more than if
We had been choked with soot.

'Ah! well a-day! what evil looks
Had I from old and young!
Instead of the cross, the Albatross
About my neck was hung.'

S. T. Coleridge (1772–1834)

The Forsaken Merman (extract)

Children dear, was it yesterday
We heard the sweet bells over the bay?
In the caverns where we lay,
Through the surf and through the swell,
The far-off sound of a silver bell?
Sand-strewn caverns, cool and deep,
Where the winds are all asleep;
Where the spent lights quiver and gleam,
Where the salt weed sways in the stream,
Where the sea-beasts, ranged all round,
Feed in the ooze of their pasture-ground;
Where the sea-snakes coil and twine,
Dry their mail and bask in the brine;
Where great whales come sailing by,
Sail and sail, with unshut eye,
Round the world for ever and aye?
When did music come this way?
Children dear, was it yesterday?

Children dear, was it yesterday
(Call yet once) that she went away?
Once she sate with you and me,
On the red gold throne in the heart of the sea,
And the youngest sate on her knee.
She comb'd its bright hair, and she tended it well,
When down swung the sound of a far-off bell.
She sigh'd, she look'd up through the clear green sea;
She said: 'I must go, for my kinsfolk pray
In the little grey church on the shore to-day.
'Twill be Easter-time in the world – ah me!
And I lose my poor soul, Merman! here with thee.
I said: 'Go up, dear heart, through the waves;
Say thy prayer, and come back to the kind sea-caves.
She smiled, she went up through the surf in the bay.
Children dear, was it yesterday?
    Children dear, were we long alone?
'The sea grows stormy, the little ones moan;
Long prayers,' I said, 'in the world they say;
Come!' I said; and we rose through the surf in the bay
We went up the beach, by the sandy down
Where the sea-stocks bloom, to the white-wall'd town
Through the narrow paved streets, where all was still,
To the little grey church on the windy hill.
From the church came a murmur of folk at their prayers
But we stood without in the cold blowing airs.
We climb'd on the graves, on the stones worn with rains
And we gazed up the aisle through the small leaded panes
She sate by the pillar; we saw her clear:
'Margaret, hist! come quick, we are here!'

Dear heart,' I said, 'we are long alone;
The sea grows stormy, the little ones moan.'
But, ah, she gave me never a look,
For her eyes were seal'd to the holy book!
Loud prays the priest; shut stands the door.
Come away, children, call no more!
Come away, come down, call no more!

Matthew Arnold
(1822–1888)

Cargoes

Quinquireme of Nineveh from distant Ophir
Rowing home to haven in sunny Palestine,
With a cargo of ivory,
And apes and peacocks,
Sandalwood, cedarwood, and sweet white wine.

Stately Spanish galleon coming from the Isthmus,
Dipping through the Tropics by the palm-green shores,
With a cargo of diamonds,
Emeralds, amethysts,
Topazes, and cinnamon, and gold moidores.

Dirty British coaster with a salt-caked smoke stack
Butting through the Channel in the mad March days,
With a cargo of Tyne coal,
Road-rail, pig-lead,
Firewood, iron-ware, and cheap tin trays.

John Masefield (1878–1967)

Goodness Gracious!

Goodness gracious, fiddle dee dee!
Somebody's grandmother out at sea!

Just where the breakers begin to bound
Somebody's grandmother bobbing around.

Up on the shore the people shout,
'Give us a hand and we'll pull you out!'

'No!' says the granny. 'I'm right as rain,
And I'm going to go on till I get to Spain.'

Margaret Mahy (1936–)

Sea

I am patient, repetitive, multi-voiced,
Yet few hear me
And fewer still trouble to understand

Why, for example, I caress
And hammer the land.
I do not brag of my depths

Or my currents, I do not
Boast of my moods or my colours
Or my breath in your thought.

In time I surrender my drowned,
My appetite speaks for itself,
I could swallow all you have found

And open for more,
My green tongues licking the shores
Of the world

Like starved beasts reaching for men
Who will not understand
When I rage and roar

When I bellow and threaten
I am obeying a law
Observing a discipline.

This is the rhythm
I live.
This is the reason I move

In hunger and skill
To give you the pick of my creatures.
This is why I am willing to kill,

Chill every created nerve.
You have made me a savage master
Because I know how to serve.

Brendan Kennelly (1936–)

The Tide in the River

The tide in the river,
The tide in the river,
The tide in the river runs deep.
I saw a shiver
Pass over the river
As the tide turned in its sleep.

Eleanor Farjeon (1881–1965)

Grim and Gloomy

Oh, grim and gloomy,
So grim and gloomy
Are the caves beneath the sea.
Oh, rare but roomy
And bare and boomy,
Those salt sea caverns be.

Oh, slim and slimy
Or grey and grimy
Are the animals of the sea.
Salt and oozy
And safe and snoozy
The caves where those animals be.

Hark to the shuffling,
Huge and snuffling,
Ravenous, cavernous, great sea-
    beasts!
But fair and fabulous,
Tintinnabulous,
Gay and fabulous are their feasts.

Ah, but the queen of the sea,
The querulous, perilous sea!
How the curls of her tresses
The pearls on her dresses,
Sway and swirl in the waves,
How cosy and dozy,
How sweet ring-a-rosy
Her bower in the deep-sea caves!

Oh, rare but roomy
And bare and boomy
Those caverns under the sea,
And grave and grandiose,
Safe and sandiose
The dens of her denizens be.

James Reeves (1909–1978)

The Wreck of the Hesperus *(extract)*

And fast through the midnight dark and drear,
Through the whistling sleet and snow,
Like a sheeted ghost the vessel swept
Towards the reef of Norman's Woe.

And ever the fitful gusts between
A sound came from the land
It was the sound of the trampling surf,
On the rocks and the hard sea–sand.

The breakers were right beneath her bows,
She drifted a dreary wreck,
And a whooping billow swept the crew
Like icicles from her deck.

She struck where the white and fleecy waves
Looked soft as carded wool,
But the cruel rocks, they gored her side
Like the horns of an angry bull.

Her rattling shrouds, all sheathed in ice,
With the masts went by the board;
Like a vessel of glass, she stove and sank,
Ho! ho! the breakers roared!

★ ★ ★

Such was the wreck of the Hesperus,
In the midnight and the snow;
Christ save us all from a death like this,
On the reef of Norman's Woe!

H. W. Longfellow (1807–1882)

Summoned by Bells
(extract from Chapter 3)

Then before breakfast down toward the sea
I ran alone, monarch of miles of sand,
Its shining stretches satin-smooth and vein'd.
I felt beneath bare feet the lugworm casts
And walked where only gulls and oyster-catchers
Had stepped before me to the water's edge.
The morning tide flowed in to welcome me,
The fan-shaped scallop shells, the backs of crabs,
The bits of driftwood worn to reptile shapes,
The heaps of bladder-wrack the tide had left
(Which, lifted up, sent sandhoppers to leap
In hundreds round me) answered 'Welcome back!'

Sir John Betjeman (1906–1984)

The Owl and the Pussy-Cat

The Owl and the Pussy-cat went to sea
  In a beautiful pea-green boat,
They took some honey, and plenty of money,
  Wrapped up in a five-pound note.
The Owl looked up to the stars above,
  And sang to a small guitar,
'O lovely Pussy! O Pussy, my love,
    What a beautiful Pussy you are,
      You are,
      You are!
    What a beautiful Pussy you are!'

Pussy said to the Owl, 'You elegant fowl!
  How charmingly sweet you sing!
O let us be married! too long we have tarried:
  But what shall we do for a ring?'
They sailed away, for a year and a day,
  To the land where the Bong-tree grows
And there in a wood a Piggy-wig stood
  With a ring at the end of his nose,
    His nose,
    His nose,
  With a ring at the end of his nose.

'Dear Pig, are you willing to sell for one shilling
   Your ring?' Said the Piggy, 'I will.'
So they took it away, and were married next day
   By the Turkey who lives on the hill.
They dined on mince, and slices of quince,
   Which they ate with a runcible spoon;
And hand in hand, on the edge of the sand,
   They danced by the light of the moon,
      The moon,
      The moon,
   They danced by the light of the moon.

Edward Lear (1812–1888)

Sir Patrick Spens

THE SAILING

The king sits in Dunfermline town
Drinking the blude-red wine;
'O where will I get a skeely skipper
To sail this new ship o' mine?'

O up and spake an eldern knight,
Sat at the king's right knee:
'Sir Patrick Spens is the best sailor
That ever sail'd the sea.'

'Our king has written a broad letter,
And seal'd it with his hand,
And sent it to Sir Patrick Spens,
Who was walking on the strand.

'To Noroway, to Noroway,
To Noroway o'er the foam;
The king's daughter o' Noroway,
'Tis thou must bring her home.'

The first word that Sir Patrick read
So loud, loud laugh'd he;
The next word that Sir Patrick read
The tear blinded his e'e.

'O who is this has done this deed
And told the king o' me,
To send us out, at this time o' year,
To sail upon the sea?

'Be it wind, be it wet, be it hail, be it sleet,
Our ship must sail the foam;
The king's daughter o' Noroway,
'Tis we must fetch her home.'

They hoisted their sails on
   Monenday morn
With all the speed they may;
They have landed in Noroway
Upon a Wednesday.

THE RETURN

*The men of Norway seem to have insulted
their Scottish guests by hinting that they were
staying too long, and this caused Sir Patrick Spens
to sail for home without waiting for fair weather.*

'Make ready, make ready, my merry men all!
Our good ship sails the morn.' –
'Now ever alack, my master dear,
I fear a deadly storm.

'I saw the new moon late yest'r-e'en
With the old moon in her arm;
And if we go to sea, master,
I fear we'll come to harm.'

They had not sail'd a league, a league,
A league but barely three,
When the lift grew dark, and the wind blew loud,
And gurly grew the sea.

The anchors brake, and the topmast lap,
It was such a deadly storm;
And the waves came o'er the broken ship
Till all her sides were torn.

'O where will I get a good sailor
To take my helm in hand,
While I go up to the tall topmast
To see if I can spy land?' –

'O here am I, a sailor good,
To take the helm in hand,
While you go up to the tall topmast,
But I fear you'll ne'er spy land.'

He had not gone a step, a step,
A step but barely one,
When a bolt flew out of our goodly ship,
And the salt sea it came in.

'Go fetch a web o' the silken cloth,
Another o' the twine,
And wap them into our ship's side,
And let not the sea come in.'

They fetch'd a web o' the silken cloth,
Another o' the twine,
And they wapp'd them round that good ship's side,
But still the sea came in.

O loth, loth were our good Scots lords
To wet their cork-heeled shoon;
But long ere all the play was play'd
They wet their hats aboon.

And many was the feather bed
That flatter'd on the foam;
And many was the good lord's son
That never more came home.

O long, long may the ladies sit,
With their fans into their hand,
Before they see Sir Patrick Spens
Come sailing to the strand!

And long, long may the maidens sit
With their gold combs in their hair,
A-waiting for their own dear loves!
For them they'll see no more.

Half-o'er, half-o'er to Aberdour,
'Tis fifty fathoms deep;
And there lies good Sir Patrick Spens,
With the Scots lords at his feet!

Anon.

I Saw Three Ships

I saw three ships come sailing by,
Come sailing by, come sailing by;
I saw three ships come sailing by,
On New Year's Day in the morning.

And what do you think was in them then,
Was in them then, was in them then?
And what do you think was in them then,
On New Year's Day in the morning?

Three pretty girls were in them then,
Were in them then, were in them then;
Three pretty girls were in them then,
On New Year's Day in the morning.

And one could whistle, and one could sing,
And one could play on the violin –
Such joy there was at my wedding,
On New Year's Day in the morning.

Anon.

now is a ship

now is a ship

which captain am
sails out of sleep

steering for dream

*E. E. Cummings
(1894–1962)*

YOUNG
& OLD

'I remember, I remember'

The Hump

The Camel's hump is an ugly lump
   Which well you may see at the Zoo;
But uglier yet is the hump we get
   From having too little to do.

Kiddies and grown-ups too-oo-oo,
If we haven't enough to do-oo-oo,
     We get the hump –
     Cameelious hump –
The hump that is black and blue!

We climb out of bed with a frouzly head,
    And a snarly-yarly voice.
We shiver and scowl and we grunt and we growl
    At our bath and our boots and our toys;

And there ought to be a corner for me
(And I know there is one for you)
        When we get the hump −
        Cameelious hump −
The hump that is black and blue!

The cure for this ill is not to sit still,
    Or frowst with a book by the fire;
But to take a large hoe and a shovel also,
    And dig till you gently perspire;

And then you will find that the sun and the wind,
And the Djinn of the Garden too,
        Have lifted the hump −
        The horrible hump −
The hump that is black and blue!

I get it as well as you-oo-oo −
If I haven't enough to do-oo-oo!
        We all get the hump −
        Cameelious hump −
Kiddies and grown-ups too!

Rudyard Kipling (1865–1936)

Giorno dei Morte (The Day of the Dead)

Along the avenue of cypresses,
All in their scarlet cloaks and surplices
Of linen, go the chanting choristers,
The priests in gold and black, the villagers . . .

And all along the path to the cemetery
The round dark heads of men crowd silently,
And black-scarved faces of womenfolk, wistfully
Watch at the banner of death, and the mystery.

And at the foot of a grave a father stands
With sunken head, and forgotten, folded hands;
And at the foot of a grave a mother kneels
With pale shut face, nor either hears nor feels

The coming of the chanting choristers
Between the avenue of cypresses,
The silence of the many villagers,
The candle-flames beside
    the surplices.

> *D. H. Lawrence (1885–1930)*

Mid-Term Break

I sat all morning in the college sick bay
Counting bells knelling classes to a close.
At two o'clock our neighbours drove me home.

In the porch I met my father crying –
He had always taken funerals in his stride –
And Big Jim Evans saying it was a hard blow.

The baby cooed and laughed and rocked the pram
When I came in, and I was embarrassed
By old men standing up to shake my hand

And tell me they were 'sorry for my trouble'.
Whispers informed strangers I was the eldest,
Away at school, as my mother held my hand

In hers and coughed out angry tearless sighs.
At ten o'clock the ambulance arrived
With the corpse, stanched and bandaged by the nurses.

Next morning I went up into the room. Snowdrops
And candles soothed the bedside; I saw him
For the first time in six weeks. Paler now,

Wearing a poppy bruise on his left temple,
He lay in the four foot box as in his cot.
No gaudy scars, the bumper knocked him clear.

A four foot box, a foot for every year.

Seamus Heaney (1939–)

Me and My Brother

Me and my brother,
we sit up in bed
doing my dad's sayings.
I go to bed first
and I'm just dozing off
and I hear a funny voice going:
'Never let me see you doing that again,'
and it's my brother
poking his finger out just like my dad
going:
'Never let me see you doing that again.'
And so I join in
and we're both going:
'Never let me see you doing that again.'

So what happens next time I get into trouble
and my dad's telling me off?
He's going:
'Never
let
me
see
you
doing
that
again.'
So I'm looking up at my dad
going,
'Sorry, Dad, sorry,'
and I suddenly catch sight of my brother's big red
face poking out from behind my dad.

And while my dad is poking me with his finger
in time with the words:
'Never
let
me
see
you
doing
that again,'
there's my brother doing just the same
behind my dad's back
just where I can see him
and he's saying the words as well
with his mouth without making a sound.

So I start laughing
and so my dad says,
'AND IT'S NO LAUGHING MATTER.'
Of course my brother knows that one as well
and he's going with his mouth:
'And it's no laughing matter.'

But my dad's not stupid.
He knows something's going on.
So he looks round
and there's my brother
with his finger poking out
just like my dad
and I'm standing there laughing.
Oh no
then we get into
REALLY BIG TROUBLE.

Michael Rosen (1946–)

Warning to Children

Children, if you dare to think
Of the greatness, rareness, muchness,
Fewness of this precious only
Endless world in which you say
You live, you think of things like this:
Blocks of slate enclosing dappled
Red and green, enclosing tawny
Yellow nets, enclosing white
And black acres of dominoes,
Where a neat brown paper parcel
Tempts you to untie the string.
In the parcel a small island,
On the island a large tree,
On the tree a husky fruit.
Strip the husk and pare the rind off:
In the kernel you will see
Blocks of slate enclosed by dappled
Red and green, enclosed by tawny
Yellow nets, enclosed by white
And black acres of dominoes,
Where the same brown paper parcel –
Children, leave the string alone!
For who dares undo the parcel
Finds himself at once inside it,
On the island, in the fruit,
Blocks of slate about his head,
Finds himself enclosed by dappled
Green and red, enclosed by yellow
Tawny nets, enclosed by black
And white acres of dominoes,

With the same brown paper parcel
Still unopened on his knee.
And, if he then should dare to think
Of the fewness, muchness, rareness,
Greatness of this endless only
Precious world in which he says
He lives – he then unties the string.

Robert Graves (1895–1985)

The Reverend Sabine Baring-Gould

The Reverend Sabine Baring-Gould,
Rector (sometime) at Lew,
Once at a Christmas party asked,
'Whose pretty child are you?'

(The Rector's family was long,
His memory was poor,
And as to who was who had grown
Increasingly unsure.)

At this, the infant on the stair
Most sorrowfully sighed.
'Whose pretty little girl am I?
Why, yours, papa!' she cried.

Charles Causley (1917–)

Betty at the Party

'When I was at the party,'
Said Betty, aged just four,
'A little girl fell off her chair
Right down upon the floor;
And all the other little girls
Began to laugh, but me –
I didn't laugh a single bit,'
Said Betty seriously.

'Why not?' her mother asked her,
Full of delight to find
That Betty – bless her little heart! –
Had been so sweetly kind.
'Why didn't you laugh, my darling?
Or don't you like to tell?'
'I didn't laugh,' said Betty,
''Cause it was me that fell.'

Anon.

Lullaby for a Naughty Girl

Oh peace, my Penelope: slaps are the fate
Of all little girls who are born to be great;
And the greatest of Queens have all been little girls
And dried up their tears on their kerchiefs or curls.

Oh sleep; and your heart that has sobbed for so long
Will mend and grow merry and wake you to song;
For the world is a lovelier place than it seems,
And a smack cannot follow you into your dreams.

The dark Cleopatra was slapped on the head,
And she wept as she lay in her great golden bed;
But the dark Cleopatra woke up with a smile
As she thought of the little boats out on the Nile.

And Helen of Troy had many a smack:
She moaned and she murmured the Greek for 'Alack!'
But the sun rose in Argos, and wonderful joy
Came with the morning to Helen of Troy.

They sent Guinevere without supper to sleep
In her grey little room at the top of the Keep;
And the stars over Camelot waited and wept
Till the peeping moon told them that Guinevere slept.

There was grief in Castile and dismay in Madrid
When they slapped Isabella for something she did;
But she slept – and could laugh in the morning again
At the Dons of Castile, the Hidalgos of Spain.

And oh, how Elizabeth cried in her cot
When she wanted her doll and her Nanny said not!
But the sparrows awoke and the summer sun rose,
And there was the doll on the bed by her toes!

So sleep, my Penelope: slaps are the fate
Of all little girls who are born to be great;
But the world is a lovelier place than it seems,
And a smack cannot follow you into your dreams.

E. V. Rieu (1887–1972)

My Mother Said

My mother said I never should
Play with the gypsies in the wood;
If I did, she would say,
Naughty girl to disobey.
Your hair shan't curl
And your shoes shan't shine,
You gypsy girl,
You shan't be mine.

And my father said that if I did
He'd rap my head with the tea-pot lid.
The wood was dark; the grass was green;
In came Sally with a tambourine.
I went to the sea – no ship to get across;
I paid ten shillings for a blind white horse;
I up on his back and was off in a crack,
Sally tell my mother I shall never come back.

Anon.

My Shadow

I have a little shadow that goes in and out with me,
And what can be the use of him is more than I can see.
He is very, very like me from the heels up to the head;
And I see him jump before me, when I jump into my bed.

The funniest thing about him is the way he likes to grow –
Not at all like proper children, which is always very slow;
For he sometimes shoots up taller like an india-rubber ball,
And he sometimes gets so little that there's none of him at all.

He hasn't got a notion of how children ought to play,
And can only make a fool of me in every sort of way.
He stays so close beside me, he's a coward you can see;
I'd think shame to stick to nursie as that shadow sticks to me!

One morning, very early, before the sun was up,
I rose and found the shining dew on every buttercup;
But my lazy little shadow, like an arrant sleepy-head,
Had stayed at home behind me and was fast asleep in bed.

R. L. Stevenson (1850–1894)

Timothy Winters

Timothy Winters comes to school
With eyes as wide as a football pool,
Ears like bombs and teeth like splinters:
A blitz of a boy is Timothy Winters.

His belly is white, his neck is dark,
And his hair is an exclamation mark.
His clothes are enough to scare a crow
And through his britches the blue winds blow.

When teacher talks he won't hear a word
And he shoots down dead the arithmetic-bird,
He licks the patterns off his plate
And he's not even heard of the Welfare State.

Timothy Winters has bloody feet
And he lives in a house on Suez Street,
He sleeps in a sack on the kitchen floor
And they say there aren't boys like him any more.

Old Man Winters likes his beer
And his missus ran off with a bombardier,
Grandma sits in the grate with a gin
And Timothy's dosed with an aspirin.

The Welfare Worker lies awake
But the law's as tricky as a ten-foot snake,
So Timothy Winters drinks his cup
And slowly goes on growing up.

At Morning Prayers the Master helves†
For children less fortunate than ourselves,
And the loudest response in the room is when
Timothy Winters roars 'Amen!'

So come one angel, come on ten:
Timothy Winters says 'Amen
Amen amen amen amen.'
Timothy Winters, Lord.

Amen

Charles Causley (1917–)

†a dialect word from north Cornwall used to describe the
alarmed lowing of cattle (as when a cow is separated from
her calf); a desperate, pleading note.

The Little Boy and the Old Mam

Said the little boy, 'Sometimes I drop my spoon.'
Said the little old man, 'I do that too.'
The little boy whispered, 'I wet my pants.'
'I do that too,' laughed the little old man.
Said the little boy, 'I often cry.'
The old man nodded, 'So do I.'
'But worst of all,' said the boy, it seems
Grown-ups don't pay attention to me.'
And he felt the warmth of a wrinkled old hand.
'I know what you mean,' said the little old man.

Shel Silverstein (1932–)

I Remember, I Remember

I remember, I remember,
The house where I was born,
The little window where the sun
Came peeping in at morn;
He never came a wink too soon,
Nor brought too long a day,
But now, I often wish the night
Had borne my breath away.

I remember, I remember,
The roses, red and white;
The violets, and the lily-cups,
Those flowers made of light!
The lilacs where the robin built,
And where my brother set
The laburnum on his birthday –
The tree is living yet!

I remember, I remember,
Where I was used to swing;
And thought the air must rush as fresh
To swallows on the wing:
My spirit flew in feathers then,
That is so heavy now,
And summer pools could hardly cool
The fever on my brow!

I remember, I remember,
The fir trees dark and high;
I used to think their slender tops
Were close against the sky:
It was a childish ignorance,
But now 'tis little joy
To know I'm farther off from Heav'n
Than when I was a boy.

Thomas Hood (1799–1845)

From a New Boy

When first I played I nearly died.
The bitter memory still rankles –
They formed a scrum with me inside!
Some kicked the ball and some my ankles.
I did not like the game at all,
Yet, after all the harm they'd done me,
Whenever I came near the ball
They knocked me down and stood upon me.

Rupert Brooke (1887–1915)

Tiger

At noon the paper tigers roar –
Miroslav Holub

The paper tigers roar at noon;
The sun is hot, the sun is high.
They roar in chorus, not in tune,
Their plaintive, savage hunting cry.

O, when you hear them, stop your ears
And clench your lids and bite your tongue.
The harmless paper tiger bears
Strong fascination for the young.

His forest is the busy street;
His dens the forum and the mart;
He drinks no blood, he tastes no meat:
He riddles and corrupts the heart.

But when the dusk begins to creep
From tree to tree, from door to door,
The jungle tiger wakes from sleep
And utters his authentic roar.

It bursts the night and shakes the stars
Till one breaks blazing from the sky;
Then listen! If to meet it soars
Your heart's reverberating cry,

My child, then put aside your fear:
Unbar the door and walk outside!
The real tiger waits you there;
His golden eyes shall be your guide.

And, should he spare you in his wrath,
The world and all the worlds are yours;
And should he leap the jungle path
And clasp you with his bloody jaws,

Then say, as his divine embrace
Destroys the mortal parts of you:
I too am of that royal race
Who do what we are born to do.

A. D. Hope (1907–1933)

Watch Your French

When my mum tipped a panful of red-hot fat
Over her foot, she did quite a little chat,
And I won't tell you what she said
But it wasn't:
'Fancy that!
I must try in future to be far more careful
With this red-hot scalding fat!'

When my dad fell over and landed – splat! –
With a trayful of drinks (he'd tripped over the cat)
I won't tell you what he said
But it wasn't:
'Fancy that!
I must try in future to be far
    more careful
To step round our splendid cat!'

When Uncle Joe brought me a
    cowboy hat
Back from the States, the dog
    stomped it flat,
And I won't tell you what I said
But Mum and Dad yelled:
'STOP THAT!
Where did you learn that
    appalling language?
Come on. Where?'

'I've no idea,' I said,
'No idea.'

Kit Wright (1944–)

Law and Justice

Now, this is Mary Queen of Scots!
Push all her curls away;
For we have heard about her plots,
And she must die to-day.

What's this? I MUST NOT HURT HER SO;
YOU LOVE HER DEARLY STILL;
YOU THINK SHE WILL BE GOOD? – Oh, no!
I say she never will.

My own new saw, and made of steel!
Oh, silly child to cry;
She's only wood, she cannot feel,
And, look, her eyes are dry.

Her cheeks are bright with rosy spots;
I know she cares for none –
Besides, she's Mary, Queen of Scots
And so it MUST be done!

Jean Ingelow (1820–1897)

Mum is Having a Baby!

Mum is having a baby!
I'm shocked! I'm all at sea!
What's she want another one for:
WHAT'S THE MATTER WITH ME!?

Colin McNaughton (1951–)

The Railway Children

When we climbed the slopes of the cutting
We were eye-level with the white cups
Of the telegraph poles and the sizzling wires.

Like lovely freehand they curved for miles
East and miles west beyond us, sagging
Under their burden of swallows.

We were small and thought we knew nothing
Worth knowing. We thought words travelled the wires
In the shiny pouches of raindrops,

Each one seeded full with the light
Of the sky, the gleam of the lines, and ourselves
So infinitesimally scaled

We could stream through the eye of a needle.

Seamus Heaney (1936–)

HEROES &
WARRIORS

'Dim drums throbbing,
in the hills half heard'

The Highwayman

The wind was a torrent of darkness among the gusty trees,
The moon was a ghostly galleon tossed upon cloudy seas,
The road was a ribbon of moonlight over the purple moor,
And the highwayman came riding –
      Riding – riding –
The highwayman came riding, up to the old inn-door.

He'd a French cocked-hat on his forehead, a bunch of lace at his chin,
A coat of claret velvet, and breeches of brown doe-skin;
They fitted with never a wrinkle: his boots were up to the thigh!
And he rode with a jewelled twinkle,
      His pistol butts a-twinkle,
His rapier hilt a-twinkle, under the jewelled sky.

Over the cobbles he clattered and clashed in the dark inn-yard,
And he tapped with his whip on the shutters, but all was locked
   and barred;
He whistled a tune to the window, and who should be
   waiting there
But the landlord's black-eyed daughter,
         Bess, the landlord's daughter,
Plaiting a dark red love-knot into her long black hair.

And dark in the old inn-yard a stable-wicket creaked
Where Tim the ostler listened; his face was white and peaked;
His eyes were hollows of madness, his hair like mouldy hay,
But he loved the landlord's daughter,
         The landlord's red-lipped daughter;
Dumb as a dog he listened, and he heard the robber say –

'One kiss, my bonny sweetheart, I'm after a prize to-night,
But I shall be back with the yellow gold before the morning light;
Yet, if they press me sharply, and harry me through the day,
Then look for me by moonlight,
         Watch for me by moonlight,
I'll come to thee by moonlight, though hell should bar the way.'

He rose upright in the stirrups; he scarce could reach her hand,
But she loosened her hair i' the casement! His face burnt like
   a brand
As the black cascade of perfume came tumbling over his breast;
And he kissed its waves in the moonlight,
         (Oh, sweet black waves in the moonlight!)
Then he tugged at his rein in the moonlight, and galloped away
   to the west.

He did not come in the dawning; he did not come at noon;
And out o' the tawny sunset, before the rise o' the moon,
When the road was a gypsy's ribbon, looping the purple moor,
A red-coat troop came marching –
   Marching – marching –
King George's men came marching, up to the old inn-door.

They said no word to the landlord, they drank his ale instead,
But they gagged his daughter and bound her to the foot of her
 narrow bed;
Two of them knelt at her casement, with muskets at their side!
There was death at every window;
   And hell at one dark window;
For Bess could see, through her casement, the road that he would ride.

They had tied her up to attention, with many a sniggering jest;
They had bound a musket beside her, with the barrel beneath
 her breast!
'Now keep good watch!' and they kissed her.
   She heard the dead man say –
Look for me by moonlight;
   Watch for me by moonlight;
I'll come to thee by moonlight, though hell should bar the way!

She twisted her hands behind her; but all the knots held good!
She writhed her hands till her fingers were wet with sweat or blood!
They stretched and strained in the darkness, and the hours crawled by
 like years,
Till, now, on the stroke of midnight,
   Cold, on the stroke of midnight,
The tip of one finger touched it! The trigger at least was hers!

The tip of one finger touched it; she strove no more for the rest!
Up, she stood to attention, with the barrel beneath her breast,
She would not risk their hearing; she would not strive again;
For the road lay bare in the moonlight;
        Blank and bare in the moonlight;
And the blood of her veins in the moonlight throbbed to her
  love's refrain.

Tlot-tlot; tlot-tlot! Had they heard it? The horse-hoofs ringing clear;
Tlot-tlot, tlot-tlot, in the distance? Were they deaf that they did not hear?
Down the ribbon of moonlight, over the brow of the hill,
The highwayman came riding,
        Riding, riding!
The red-coats looked to their priming! She stood up, straight and still!

Tlot-tlot, in the frosty silence! tlot-tlot, in the echoing night!
Nearer he came and nearer! Her face was like a light!
Her eyes grew wide for a moment; she drew one last deep breath,
Then her finger moved in the moonlight,
        Her musket shattered the moonlight,
Shattered her breast in the moonlight and warned him – with
  her death.

He turned; he spurred to the westward; he did not know who stood
Bowed, with her head o'er the musket, drenched with her own
  red blood!
Not till the dawn he heard it, and slowly blanched to hear
How Bess, the landlord's daughter,
        The landlord's black-eyed daughter,
Had watched for her love in the moonlight, and died in the
  darkness there.

Back, he spurred like a madman, shrieking a curse to the sky,
With the white road smoking behind him and his rapier brandished high!
Blood-red were his spurs i' the golden noon; wine-red was his velvet coat;
When they shot him down on the highway,
       Down like a dog on the highway,
And he lay in his blood on the highway, with the bunch of lace at his throat.

And still of a winter's night, they say, when the wind is in the trees,
When the moon is a ghostly galleon tossed upon cloudy seas,
When the road is a ribbon of moonlight over the purple moor,
A highwayman comes riding –
       Riding – riding –
A highwayman comes riding, up to the old inn-door.

Over the cobbles he clatters and clangs in the dark inn-yard
And he taps with his whip on the shutters, but all is locked and barred;
He whistles a tune to the window, and who should be waiting there
But the landlord's black-eyed daughter,
       Bess, the landlord's daughter,
Plaiting a dark red love-knot into her long black hair.

Alfred Noyes (1880–1958)

Drake's Drum

Drake he's in his hammock an' a thousand mile away,
  (Capten, art tha sleepin' there below?),
Slung atween the round shot in Nombre Dios Bay,
  An' dreamin' arl the time o' Plymouth Hoe.
Yarnder lumes the Island, yarnder lie the ships,
  Wi' sailor lads a-dancin' heel-an'-toe,
An' the shore-lights flashin', an' the night-tide dashin',
  He sees et arl so plainly as he saw et long ago.

Drake he was a Devon man, an' rüled the Devon seas,
  (Capten, art tha sleepin' there below?),
Rovin' tho' his death fell, he went wi' heart at ease,
  An' dreamin' arl the time o' Plymouth Hoe.
'Take my drum to England, hang et by the shore,
  Strike et when your powder's runnin' low;
If the Dons sight Devon, I'll quit the port o' Heaven,
  An' drum them up the Channel as we drummed them long ago.'

Drake he's in his hammock till the great Armadas come,
  (Capten, art tha sleepin' there below?),
Slung atween the round shot, listenin' for the drum,
  An' dreamin' arl the time o' Plymouth Hoe.
Call him on the deep sea, call him up the Sound,
  Call him when ye sail to meet the foe;
Where the old trade's plyin' an' the old flag flyin'
  They shall find him ware an' wakin', as they found him long ago!

Sir Henry Newbolt (1862–1938)

Lepanto *(extract)*

White founts falling in the Courts of the sun,
And the Soldan of Byzantium is smiling as they run;
There is laughter like the fountains in that face of all men feared,
It stirs the forest darkness, the darkness of his beard,
It curls the blood-red crescent, the crescent of his lips,
For the inmost sea of all the earth is shaken with his ships.
They have dared the white republics up the capes of Italy,
They have dashed the Adriatic round the Lion of the Sea,
And the Pope has cast his arms abroad for agony and loss,
And called the kings of Christendom for swords about the Cross.
The cold queen of England is looking in the glass;
The shadow of the Valois is yawning at the Mass;
From evening isles fantastical rings faint the Spanish gun,
And the Lord upon the Golden Horn is laughing in the sun.

Dim drums throbbing, in the hills half heard,
Where only on a nameless throne a crownless prince
   has stirred,
Where, risen from a doubtful seat and half attainted stall,
The last knight of Europe takes weapons from the wall,
The last and lingering troubadour to whom the bird has sung,
That once went singing southward when all the world
   was young.
In that enormous silence, tiny and unafraid,
Comes up along a winding road the noise of the Crusade.
Strong gongs groaning as the guns boom far,
Don John of Austria is going to the war,
Stiff flags straining in the night-blasts cold
In the gloom black-purple, in the glint old-gold,
Torchlight crimson on the copper kettle-drums,
Then the tuckets, then the trumpets, then the cannon,
   and he comes.
Don John laughing in the brave beard curled,
Spurning of his stirrups like the thrones of all the world,
Holding his head up for a flag of all the free.
Love-light of Spain – hurrah!
Death-light of Africa!
Don John of Austria
Is riding to the sea.

                      G. K. Chesterton (1874–1936)

Lochinvar

O, young Lochinvar has come out of the west,
Through all the wide Border, his steed was the best;
And save his good broadsword he weapons had none,
He rode all unarm'd and he rode all alone.
   So faithful in love and so dauntless in war,
   There never was knight like the young Lochinvar.

He staid not for brake, and he stopp'd not for stone,
He swam the Eske river where ford there was none;
But ere he alighted at Netherby gate,
The bride had consented; the gallant came late:
   For a laggard in love and a dastard in war,
   Was to wed the fair Ellen of brave Lochinvar.

So boldly he enter'd the Netherby Hall,
Among bride's-men and kinsmen and brothers and all:
Then spoke the bride's father, his hand on his sword,
(For the poor craven bridegroom said never a word),
   'O come ye in peace here, or come ye in war,
   Or to dance at our bridal, young Lord Lochinvar?'

'I long woo'd your daughter, my suit you denied;
Love swells like the Solway, but ebbs like its tide –
And now am I come, with this lost love of mine,
To lead but one measure, drink one cup of wine.
   There are maidens in Scotland more lovely by far,
   That would gladly be bride to the young Lochinvar.

The bride kiss'd the goblet: the knight took it up,
He quaff'd off the wine, and he threw down the cup.
She look'd down to blush and she look'd up to sigh,
With a smile on her lips, and a tear in her eye.
   He took her soft hand ere her mother could bar,
   'Now tread me a measure!' said young Lochinvar.

So stately his form, and so lovely her face,
That never a hall such a galliard did grace;
While her mother did fret, and her father did fume,
And the bridegroom stood dangling his bonnet and plume;
    And the bride-maidens whispered, ''Twere better by far,
    To have matched our fair cousin with young Lochinvar.'

One touch to her hand, and one word in her ear,
When they reach'd the hall-door, and the charger stood near;
So light to the croupe the fair lady he swung,
So light to the saddle before her he sprung!
    'She is won! We are gone, over bank, bush and scaur;
    They'll have fleet steeds that follow!' quoth young Lochinvar.

There was mounting 'mong Graemes of the Netherby clan;
Forsters, Fenwicks and Musgraves, they rode and they ran:
There was racing and chasing, on Cannobie Lee,
But the lost bride of Netherby ne'er did they see.
   So daring in love, and so dauntless in war,
   Have ye e'er heard of gallant like young Lochinvar?

Sir Walter Scott (1771–1832)

The Lion and the Unicorn

The lion and the unicorn
Were fighting for the crown;
The lion beat the unicorn
All round the town.

Some gave them white bread,
And some gave them brown;
Some gave them plum-cake,
And drummed them out of town.

Anon.

'Over the heather the wet wind blows'

Over the heather the wet wind blows,
I've lice in my tunic and a cold in my nose.

The rain comes pattering out of the sky,
I'm a Wall soldier, I don't know why.

The mist creeps over the hard grey stone,
My girl's in Tungria; I sleep alone.

Aulus goes hanging around her place,
I don't like his manners, I don't like his face.

Piso's a Christian, he worships a fish;
There'd be no kissing if he had his wish.

She gave me a ring but I diced it away,
I want my girl and I want my pay.

When I'm a veteran with only one eye
I shall do nothing but look at the sky.

W. H. Auden (1907–1973)

Tweedle-dum and Tweedle-dee

Tweedle-dum and Tweedle-dee
Resolved to have a battle
For Tweedle-dum said Tweedle-dee
Had spoiled his nice new rattle.

Just then flew by a monstrous crow
As big as a tar-barrel,
Which frightened both the heroes so
They quite forgot their quarrel.

Anon.

A Smugglers' Song

If you wake at midnight and hear a horse's feet,
Don't go drawing back the blind, or looking in the street,
Them that asks no questions isn't told a lie.
Watch the wall, my darling, while the Gentlemen go by!
　　　　　Five and twenty ponies,
　　　　　Trotting through the dark –
　　　　　Brandy for the Parson,
　　　　　'Baccy for the Clerk;
　　　　　Laces for a lady; letters for a spy,
And watch the wall, my darling, while the Gentlemen go by!

Running round the woodlump if you chance to find
Little barrels, roped and tarred, all full of brandy-wine;
Don't you shout to come and look, nor take 'em for your play;
Put the brushwood back again, – and they'll be gone next day!

If you see the stableyard setting open wide;
If you see a tired horse lying down inside;
If your mother mends a coat cut about and tore;
If the lining's wet and warm – don't you ask no more!

If you meet King George's men, dressed in blue and red,
You be careful what you say, and mindful what is said.
If they call you 'pretty maid', and chuck you 'neath the chin,
Don't you tell where no one is, nor yet where no one's been!

Knocks and footsteps round the house – whistles after dark –
You've no call for running out till the housedogs bark.
Trusty's here and Pincher's here, and see how dumb they lie –
They don't fret to follow when the Gentlemen go by!

If you do as you've been told, likely there's a chance,
You'll be give a dainty doll, all the way from France,
With a cap of Valenciennes, and a velvet hood –
A present from the Gentlemen, along o' being good!
   Five and twenty ponies,
   Trotting through the dark –
   Brandy for the Parson,
   'Baccy for the Clerk.
Them that asks no questions isn't told a lie –
Watch the wall, my darling, while the Gentlemen go by!

Rudyard Kipling (1865–1936)

The Other Little Boats: July 1588

A pause came in the fighting and England held her breath
For the battle was not ended and the ending might be death.
Then out they came, the little boats, from all the Channel shore
Free men were these who set the sails and laboured at the oars.
From Itchenor and Shoreham, from Deal and Winchelsea,
They put out into the Channel to keep their country free.
Not of Dunkirk this story, but of boatmen long ago,
When our Queen was Gloriana and King Philip was our foe
And galleons rode the Narrow Sea, and Effingham and Drake
Were out of shot and powder, with all England still at stake.
They got the shot and powder, they charged their guns again,
The guns that guarded England from the galleons of Spain,
And the men who helped them to do it, helped them still to hold the sea
Men from Itchenor and Shoreham, men from Deal and Winchelsea,
Looked out happily from Heaven and cheered to see the work
Of their grandsons' grandsons' grandsons on the beaches of Dunkirk.

Edward Shanks (1892–1953)

Discovery

There was an Indian, who had known no change,
Who strayed content along a sunlit beach
Gathering shells. He heard a sudden strange
Commingled noise; looked up; and gasped for speech.
For in the bay, where nothing was before,
Moved on the sea, by magic, huge canoes,
With bellying cloths on poles, and not one oar,
And fluttering coloured signs and clambering crews.
And he, in fear, this naked man alone,
His fallen hands forgetting all their shells,
His lips gone pale, knelt low behind a stone,
And stared, and saw, and did not understand,
Columbus's doom-burdened caravels'†   †kind of sailing ship
Slant to the shore, and all their seamen land.

Sir John Squire (1884–1958)

The Dying Airman

A handsome young airman lay dying,
And as on the aerodrome he lay,
To the mechanics who round him came sighing,
The last dying words he did say:

'Take the cylinders out of my kidneys,
The connecting-rod out of my brain,
Take the cam-shaft from out of my backbone,
And assemble the engine again.'

Anon.

Excelsior

The shades of night were falling fast,
As through an Alpine village passed
A youth, who bore, 'mid snow and ice,
A banner with the strange device,
  Excelsior!

His brow was sad; his eye beneath
Flashed like a faulchion from its sheath,
And like a silver clarion rung
The accents of that unknown tongue,
  Excelsior!

In happy homes he saw the light
Of household fires gleam warm and bright;
Above, the spectral glaciers shone,
And from his lips escaped a groan,
  Excelsior!

'Try not the Pass!' the old man said,
'Dark lowers the tempest overhead,
The roaring torrent is deep and wide!'
And loud that clarion voice replied,
  Excelsior!

'O stay!' the maiden said, 'and rest
Thy weary head upon this breast!'
A tear stood in his bright blue eye,
But still he answered, with a sigh,
   Excelsior!

'Beware the pine-tree's withered branch!
Beware the awful avalanche!'
This was the peasant's last goodnight!
A voice replied, far up the height,
   Excelsior!

At break of day, as heavenward
The pious monks of Saint Bernard
Uttered the oft-repeated prayer,
A voice cried through the startled air,
   Excelsior!

A traveller, by the faithful hound,
Half-buried in the snow, was found,
Still grasping in his hand of ice
That banner, with the strange device
   Excelsior!

There, in the twilight cold and grey,
Lifeless, but beautiful, he lay,
And from the sky, serene, and far,
A voice fell, like a falling star,
   Excelsior!

H. W. Longfellow (1807–1882)

Futility

Move him into the sun –
Gently its touch awoke him once,
At home, whispering of fields unsown.
Always it woke him, even in France,
Until this morning and this snow.
If anything might rouse him now
The kind old sun will know.

Think how it wakes the seeds, –
Woke, once, the clays of a cold star.
Are limbs so dear-achieved, are sides,
Full-nerved, – still warm, – too hard to stir?
Was it for this the clay grew tall?
– O what made fatuous sunbeams toil
To break earth's sleep at all?

Wilfred Owen (1893–1918)

LOVE & FRIENDSHIP

*'A frog he would
a wooing go'*

Scarborough Fair

Where are you going? To Scarborough Fair?
Parsley, sage, rosemary and thyme,
Remember me to a bonny lass there,
For once she was a true lover of mine.

Tell her to make me a cambric shirt,
Parsley, sage, rosemary and thyme,
Without any needle or thread work'd in it,
And she shall be a true lover of mine.

Tell her to wash it in yonder well,
Parsley, sage, rosemary and thyme,
Where water ne'er sprung nor a drop of rain fell,
And she shall be a true lover of mine.

Tell her to plough me an acre of land,
Parsley, sage, rosemary and thyme,
Between the sea and the salt sea strand,
And she shall be a true lover of mine.

Tell her to plough it with one ram's horn,
Parsley, sage, rosemary and thyme,
And sow it all over with one peppercorn,
And she shall be a true lover of mine.

Tell her to reap it with a sickle of leather,
Parsley, sage, rosemary and thyme,
And tie it all up with a tom tit's feather,
And she shall be a true lover of mine.

Tell her to gather it all in a sack,
Parsley, sage, rosemary and thyme,
And carry it home on a butterfly's back,
And then she shall be a true lover of mine.

Anon.

Annabel Lee

It was many and many a year ago,
    In a kingdom by the sea,
That a maiden there lived whom you may know
    By the name of Annabel Lee;
And this maiden she lived with no other thought
    Than to love and be loved by me.

I was a child and she was a child,
    In this kingdom by the sea;
But we loved with a love that was more than love –
    I and my Annabel Lee;
With a love that the wingèd seraphs of heaven
    Coveted her and me.

And this was the reason that, long ago,
    In this kingdom by the sea,
A wind blew out of a cloud, chilling
    My beautiful Annabel Lee;
So that her high born kinsmen came
    And bore her away from me,
To shut her up in a sepulchre
    In this kingdom by the sea.

The angels, not half so happy in heaven,
    Went envying her and me –
Yes! – that was the reason (as all men know,
    In this kingdom by the sea)
That the wind came out of the cloud by night,
    Chilling and killing my Annabel Lee.

But our love it was stronger by far than the love
    Of those who were older than we –
    Of many far wiser than we –
And neither the angels in heaven above,
    Nor the demons down under the sea,
Can ever dissever my soul from the soul
    Of the beautiful Annabel Lee.

For the moon never beams without bringing me dreams
    Of the beautiful Annabel Lee;
And the stars never rise but I feel the bright eyes
    Of the beautiful Annabel Lee;
And so, all the night-tide, I lie down by the side
Of my darling – my darling – my life and my bride,
    In the sepulchre there by the sea,
    In her tomb by the sounding sea.

Edgar Allan Poe (1809–1849)

Companions; A Tale of a Grandfather

I know not of what we ponder'd
Or made pretty pretence to talk,
As, her hand within mine, we wander'd
Tow'rd the pool by the limetree walk,
While the dew fell in showers from the passion flowers
And the blush-rose bent on her stalk.

I cannot recall her figure:
Was it regal as Juno's own?
Or only a trifle bigger
Than the elves who surround the throne
Of the Faery Queen, and are seen, I ween,
By mortals in dreams alone?

What her eyes were like, I know not:
Perhaps they were blurr'd with tears;
And perhaps in your skies there
    glow not
(On the contrary) clearer spheres.
No! as to her eyes I am just as wise
As you or the cat, my dears.

Her teeth, I presume, were 'pearly':
But which was she,
    brunette or blonde?
Her hair, was it quaintly curly,
Or as straight as a beadle's wand?
That I fail'd to remark: –
    it was rather dark
And shadowy round the pond.

Then the hand that reposed so snugly
In mine – was it plump or spare?
Was the countenance fair or ugly?
Nay, children, you have me there!
My eyes were p'raps blurr'd: and besides I'd heard
That it's horribly rude to stare.

And I – was I brusque and surly?
Or oppressively bland and fond?
Was I partial to rising early?
Or why did we twain abscond,
All breakfastless too, from the public view
To prowl by a misty pond?

What pass'd, what was felt or spoken –
Whether anything pass'd at all –
And whether the heart was broken
That beat under that shelt'ring shawl –
(If shawl she had on, which I doubt) – has gone,
Yes, gone from me past recall.

Was I haply the lady's suitor?
Or her uncle? I can't make out –
Ask your governess, dears, or tutor.
For myself, I'm in hopeless doubt
As to why we were there, who on earth we were,
And what this is all about.

C. S. Calverley (1831–1884)

Clementine

Oh my darling, oh my darling,
Oh my darling Clementine!
Thou are lost and gone forever,
Oh my darling, Clementine.

In a cavern, in a canyon,
Excavating for a mine,
Lived a miner, forty-niner,
And his daughter, Clementine.

Light she was and like a fairy,
And her shoes were number nine,
Herring boxes without topses
Sandals were for Clementine.

Drove she ducklings to the water
Every morning just at nine.
Hit her foot against a splinter,
Fell into the foaming brine.

Saw her lips above the water
Blowing bubbles mighty fine.
But alas! I was no swimmer,
So I lost my Clementine.

How I missed her, how I missed her,
How I missed my Clementine.
But I kissed her little sister
And forgot my Clementine.

Oh my darling, oh my darling,
Oh my darling Clementine!
Thou art lost and gone forever,
Dreadful sorry, Clementine.

Anon.

Susan Simpson

Sudden swallows swiftly skimming,
Sunset's slowly spreading shade,
Silvery songsters sweetly singing
Summer's soothing serenade.

Susan Simpson strolled sedately,
Stifling sobs, suppressing sighs.
Seeing Stephen Slocum, stately
She stopped, showing some
   surprise.

'Say', said Stephen, 'sweetest sigher;
Say, shall Stephen spouseless stay?'
Susan, seeming somewhat shyer,
Showed submissiveness
   straightway.

Summer's season slowly stretches,
Susan Simpson Slocum she –
So she signed some simple
   sketches –
Soul sought soul successfully.

★ ★ ★

Six Septembers Susan swelters;
Six sharp seasons snow supplies;
Susan's satin sofa shelters
Six small Slocums side by side.

Anon.

Poem to her Daughter (extract)

Daughter, take this amulet
tie it with cord and caring
I'll make you a chain of coral and pearl
to glow on your neck. I'll dress you nobly.
A gold clasp too – fine, without flaw
to keep with you always.
When you bathe, sprinkle perfume, and weave your
   hair in braids.
String jasmine for the counterpane.
Wear your clothes like a bride.
for your feet anklets, bracelets for your arms . . .
Don't forget rosewater,
don't forget henna for the palms of your hands.

Mwana Kupona Msham (1810–1860)

The Lady of Shalott

I
On either side the river lie
Long fields of barley and of rye,
That clothe the wold and meet the sky;
And thro' the field the road runs by
   To many-tower'd Camelot;
And up and down the people go,
Gazing where the lilies blow
Round an island there below,
   The island of Shalott.

Willows whiten, aspens quiver,
Little breezes dusk and shiver
Thro' the wave that runs for ever
By the island in the river
   Flowing down to Camelot.
Four gray walls, and four gray towers,
Overlook a space of flowers,
And the silent isle imbowers
   The Lady of Shalott.

By the margin, willow-veil'd,
Slide the heavy barges trail'd
By slow horses; and unhail'd
The shallop flitteth silken-sail'd
   Skimming down to Camelot:
But who hath seen her wave her hand?
Or at the casement seen her stand?
Or is she known in all the land,
   The Lady of Shalott?

Only reapers, reaping early
In among the bearded barley,
Hear a song that echoes cheerly
From the river winding clearly,
    Down to tower'd Camelot;
And by the moon the reaper weary,
Piling sheaves in uplands airy,
Listening, whispers ''Tis the fairy
    Lady of Shalott.'

II
There she weaves by night and day
A magic web with colours gay.
She has heard a whisper say,
A curse is on her if she stay
   To look down to Camelot.
She knows not what the curse may be,
And so she weaveth steadily,
And little other care hath she,
   The Lady of Shalott.

And moving thro' a mirror clear
That hangs before her all the year,
Shadows of the world appear.
There she sees the highway near
   Winding down to Camelot:
There the river eddy whirls,
And there the surly village-churls,
And the red cloaks of market girls,
   Pass onward from Shalott.

Sometimes a troop of damsels glad,
An abbot on an ambling pad,
Sometimes a curly shepherd-lad,
Or long-hair'd page in crimson clad,
   Goes by to tower'd Camelot;
And sometimes thro' the mirror blue
The knights come riding two and two:
She hath no loyal knight and true,
   The Lady of Shalott.

But in her web she still delights
To weave the mirror's magic sights,
For often thro' the silent nights
A funeral, with plumes and lights,
   And music, went to Camelot:
Or when the moon was overhead,
Came two young lovers lately wed;
'I am half sick of shadows,' said
   The Lady of Shalott.

III

A bow-shot from her bower-eaves,
He rode between the barley-sheaves,
The sun came dazzling thro' the leaves,
And flamed upon the brazen greaves
   Of bold Sir Lancelot.
A red-cross knight for ever kneel'd
To a lady in his shield,
That sparkled on the yellow field,
   Beside remote Shalott.

The gemmy bridle glitter'd free,
Like to some branch of stars we see
Hung in the golden Galaxy.
The bridle bells rang merrily
   As he rode down to Camelot:
And from his blazon'd baldric slung
A mighty silver bugle hung,
And as he rode his armour rung,
   Beside remote Shalott.

All in the blue unclouded weather
Thick-jewell'd shone the saddle-leather,
The helmet and the helmet-feather
Burn'd like one burning flame together,
    As he rode down to Camelot.
As often thro' the purple night,
Below the starry clusters bright,
Some bearded meteor, trailing light,
    Moves over still Shalott.

His broad clear brow in sunlight glow'd;
On burnish'd hooves his war-horse trode;
From underneath his helmet flow'd
His coal-black curls as on he rode,
    As he rode down to Camelot.
From the bank and from the river
He flash'd into the crystal mirror,
'Tirra lirra,' by the river
    Sang Sir Lancelot.

She left the web, she left the loom,
She made three paces thro' the room,
She saw the water-lily bloom.
She saw the helmet and the plume,
  She look'd down to Camelot.
Out flew the web and floated wide;
The mirror crack'd from side to side;
'The curse is come upon me!' cried
  The Lady of Shalott.

IV
In the stormy east-wind straining,
The pale yellow woods were waning,
The broad stream in his banks complaining,
Heavily the low sky raining
  Over tower'd Camelot;
Down she came and found a boat
Beneath the willow left afloat,
And round about the prow she wrote
  The Lady of Shalott.

And down the river's dim expanse –
Like some bold seer in a trance,
Seeing all his own mischance –
With a glassy countenance
  Did she look to Camelot.
And at the closing of the day,
She loosed the chain, and down she lay;
The broad stream bore her far away,
  The Lady of Shalott.

Lying, robed in snowy white
That loosely flew to left and right –
The leaves upon her falling light –
Thro' the noises of the night
  She floated down to Camelot:
And as the boat-head wound along
The willowy hills and fields among,
They heard her singing her last song,
  The Lady of Shalott.

Heard a carol, mournful, holy,
Chanted loudly, chanted lowly,
Till her blood was frozen slowly,
And her eyes were darken'd wholly,
  Turn'd to tower'd Camelot;
For ere she reach'd upon the tide
The first house by the water-side,
Singing in her song she died,
  The Lady of Shalott.

Under tower and balcony,
By garden wall and gallery,
A gleaming shape she floated by,
Dead-pale between the houses high,
   Silent into Camelot.
Out upon the wharfs they came,
Knight and burgher, lord and dame,
And round the prow they read her name,
   The Lady of Shalott.

Who is this? and what is here?
And in the lighted palace near
Died the sound of royal cheer;
And they cross'd themselves for fear,
   All the Knights at Camelot:
But Lancelot mused a little space;
He said, 'She has a lovely face;
God in His mercy lend her grace,
   The Lady of Shalott.'

Alfred, Lord Tennyson (1809–1892)

The Song of Wandering Aengus

I went out to the hazel wood,
Because a fire was in my head,
And cut and peeled a hazel wand,
And hooked a berry to a thread;
And when white moths were on the wing,
And moth-like stars were flickering out,
I dropped the berry in a stream
And caught a little silver trout.

When I had laid it on the floor
I went to blow the fire aflame,
But something rustled on the floor,
And some one called me by my name:
It had become a glimmering girl
With apple blossom in her hair
Who called me by my name and ran
And faded through the brightening air.

Though I am old with wandering
Through hollow lands and hilly lands,
I will find out where she has gone,
And kiss her lips and take her hands;
And walk among long dappled grass,
And pluck till time and times are done
The silver apples of the moon,
The golden apples of the sun.

W. B. Yeats (1865–1939)

'Where are you going to, my pretty maid?'

'Where are you going to, my pretty maid?'
'I'm going a-milking, sir,' she said.

'May I go with you, my pretty maid?'
'You're kindly welcome, sir,' she said.

'What is your father, my pretty maid?'
'My father's a farmer, sir,' she said.

'What is your fortune, my pretty maid?'
'My face is my fortune, sir,' she said.

'Then I can't marry you, my pretty maid!'
'Nobody asked you, sir,' she said.

Anon.

So We'll Go No More A-Roving

So we'll go no more a-roving
So late into the night,
Though the heart be still as loving,
And the moon be still as bright.

For the sword outwears its sheath,
And the soul wears out the breast,
And the heart must pause to breathe,
And love itself have rest.

Though the night was made for loving,
And the day returns too soon,
Yet we'll go no more a-roving
By the light of the moon.

George Gordon, Lord Byron (1788–1824)

My Baby Has No Name Yet

My baby has no name yet;
like a new-born chick or puppy,
my baby is not named yet.

What numberless texts I examined
at dawn and night and evening over again!
But not one character did I find
which is as lovely as the child.
Starry field of the sky,
or heap of pearls in the depth.
Where can the name be found, how can I?

My baby has no name yet;
like an unnamed bluebird or white flowers
from the farthest land for the first,
I have no name for this baby of ours.

Kim Nam-Jo
translated from the Korean by Ko Won

Daisy

Daisy, Daisy,
Give me your answer do,
I'm half crazy
All for the love of you;
It won't be a stylish marriage,
For I can't afford a carriage –
But you'll look sweet
Upon the seat
Of a bicycle made for two!

Anon.

A Frog He Would a Wooing Go

A Frog he would a wooing go,
Heigho, says Rowley,
Whether his mother would let him or no,
With a rowley, powley, gammon and spinach,
Heigho, says Anthony Rowley!

So off he sets in his opera hat,
Heigho, says Rowley,
And on the road he met with a rat,
With a rowley, powley, gammon and spinach,
Heigho, says Anthony Rowley!

'Pray, Mr Rat, will you go with me,'
Heigho, says Rowley,
'Kind Mrs Mousey for to see?'
With a rowley, powley, gammon and spinach,
Heigho, says Anthony Rowley!

When they came to the door of Mousey's Hall,
Heigho, says Rowley,
They gave a loud knock, and they gave a loud call.
With a rowley, powley, gammon and spinach,
Heigho, says Anthony Rowley!

'Pray, Mrs Mouse, are you within?'
Heigho, says Rowley,
'Oh, yes, kind sirs, I'm sitting to spin.'
With a rowley, powley, gammon and spinach,
Heigho, says Anthony Rowley!

'Pray, Mrs Mouse, will you give us some beer?'
Heigho, says Rowley,
'For Froggy and I are fond of good cheer.'
With a rowley, powley, gammon and spinach,
Heigho, says Anthony Rowley!

'Pray, Mr Frog, will you give us a song?'
Heigho, says Rowley,
'But let it be something that's not very long.'
With a rowley, powley, gammon and spinach,
Heigho, says Anthony Rowley!

But while they were all a merry-making,
Heigho, says Rowley,
A cat and her kittens came tumbling in.
With a rowley, powley, gammon and spinach,
Heigho, says Anthony Rowley.

The cat she seized the rat by the crown;
Heigho, says Rowley,
The kittens they pulled the little mouse down.
With a rowley, powley, gammon and spinach,
Heigho, says Anthony Rowley.

This put Mr Frog in a terrible fright,
Heigho, says Rowley,
He took up his hat, and wished them good night.
With a rowley, powley, gammon and spinach,
Heigho, says Anthony Rowley.

But as Froggy was crossing over a brook,
Heigho, says Rowley,
A lily-white duck came and swallowed him up.
With a rowley, powley, gammon and spinach,
Heigho, says Anthony Rowley.

Anon.

Vain and Careless

Lady, lovely lady,
Careless and gay!
Once when a beggar called
She gave her child away.

The beggar took the baby,
Wrapped it in a shawl,
'Bring her back,' the lady said,
'Next time you call.'

Hard by lived a vain man,
So vain and proud,
He walked on stilts
To be seen by the crowd.

Up above the chimney pots,
Tall as a mast,
And all the people ran about
Shouting till he passed.

'A splendid match surely,'
Neighbours saw it plain,
'Although she is so careless,
Although he is so vain.'

But the lady played bobcherry,
Did not see or care,
As the vain man went by her
Aloft in the air.

This gentle-born couple
Lived and died apart.
Water will not mix with oil
Nor vain with careless heart.

Robert Graves (1895–1985)

Soldier, Soldier,
Will You Marry Me?

Oh, soldier, soldier, will you marry me,
With your musket, fife and drum?
    Oh no, pretty maid, I cannot marry you,
    For I have no coat to put on.

Then away she went to the tailor's shop
As fast as legs could run,
And bought him one of the very very best,
And the soldier put it on.

Oh, soldier, soldier, will you marry me,
With your musket, fife, and drum?
    Oh no, pretty maid, I cannot marry you,
    For I have no shoes to put on.

Then away she went to the cobbler's shop
As fast as legs could run,
And bought him a pair of the very very best,
And the soldier put them on.

Oh, soldier, soldier, will you marry me,
With your musket, fife and drum?
    Oh no, pretty maid, I cannot marry you,
    For I have a wife at home.

Anon.

Give Yourself A Hug

Give yourself a hug
when you feel unloved

Give yourself a hug
when people put on airs
to make you feel a bug

Give yourself a hug
when everyone seems to give you
a cold-shoulder shrug

Give yourself a hug –
a big big hug

And keep on singing,
'Only one in a million like me
Only one in a million-billion-trillion-zillion
like me.'

Grace Nichols (1950–)

ODDS &
ENDS

*'The Wraggle Taggle
Gypsies, O!'*

Aerobics

Bend and stretch,
Stretch and bend,
Bend and stretch all day;
Squat down small,
Jump up tall,
What a game to play!
Though I'm young and beautiful,
I feel old and grey,
I'm sure it isn't natural
To exercise this way.

One and two,
Two and one,
One and two and three;
Up and down
Like a clown,
Oh, my aching knee!
If you want an easy life,
Take a tip from me:
A princess in a pop-up book
Is not the thing to be.

Richard Edwards (1949–)

The Sluggard

'Tis the voice of the Sluggard: I heard him complain,
'You have waked me too soon, I must slumber again.'
As the door on its hinges, so he on his bed
Turns his sides and his shoulders and his heavy head.

'A little more sleep, and a little more slumber',
Thus he wastes half his days, and his hours without number;
And when he gets up, he sits folding his hands,
Or walks about saunt'ring, or trifling he stands.

I passed by his garden, and saw the wild brier,
The thorn and the thistle grow broader and higher;
The clothes that hang on him are turning to rags;
And his money still wastes, till he starves or he begs.

I made him a visit, still hoping to find
That he took better care for improving his mind;
He told me his dreams, talked of eating and drinking,
But he scarce reads his Bible, and never loves thinking.

Said I then to my heart: 'Here's a lesson for me;
That man's but a picture of what I might be;
But thanks to my friends for their care in my breeding,
Who taught me betimes to love working and reading.'

Isaac Watts (1674–1748)

'He slept beneath the moon'

He slept beneath the moon
He basked beneath the sun;
He lived a life of going to do
And died with nothing done.

James Albery (1838–1889)

Reflections

The mirror above my fireplace reflects the reflected
Room in my window; I look in the mirror at night
And see two rooms, the first where left is right
And the second, beyond the reflected window, corrected
But there I am standing back to my back. The standard
Lamp comes thrice in my mirror, twice in my window,
The fire in the mirror lies two rooms away through the window,
The fire in the window lies one room away down the terrace,
My actual room stands sandwiched between confections
Of night and lights and glass and in both directions
I can see beyond and through the reflections the street lamps
At home outdoors where my indoors rooms lie stranded,
Where a taxi perhaps will drive in through the bookcase
Whose books are not for reading and past the fire
Which gives no warmth and pull up by my desk
At which I cannot write since I am not lefthanded.

Louis MacNeice (1907–1963)

Solomon Grundy

Solomon Grundy,
Born on a Monday,
Christened on Tuesday,
Married on Wednesday,
Took ill on Thursday,
Worse on Friday,
Died on Saturday,
Buried on Sunday.
That was the end
Of Solomon Grundy.

Anon.

The Pet Wig

Our teacher has a pet wig,
Nobody knows its name,
It clings to his baldy head
And looks extremely tame.

It's very calm and patient.
When dogs are on the prowl
It pretends it cannot hear the way
They clear their throats and growl.

It comes from a far-off land
(Or so we like to think),
A strange, endangered species
That's just about extinct.

After school he takes it off
And offers it some milk.
He strokes it extra gently
(Its fur is smooth as silk).

And in his lonely room at night
When he decides to retire,
He lays the wig quite carefully
On a blanket near the fire,

Where after a long day clinging
It rests content and purring.

Brian Patten (1946–)

Night Mail

This is the night mail crossing the border,
Bringing the cheque and the postal order,
Letters for the rich, letters for the poor,
The shop at the corner and the girl next door.
Pulling up Beattock, a steady climb —
The gradient's against her, but she's on time.

Past cotton grass and moorland boulder
Shovelling white steam over her shoulder,
Snorting noisily as she passes
Silent miles of wind-bent grasses.
Birds turn their heads as she approaches,
Stare from the bushes at her blank-faced coaches.

Sheep dogs cannot turn her course,
They slumber on with paws across.
In the farm she passes no one wakes,
But a jug in the bedroom gently shakes.

Dawn freshens, the climb is done.
Down towards Glasgow she descends
Towards the steam tugs yelping down the
   glade of cranes,
Towards the fields of apparatus, the furnaces
Set on the dark plain like gigantic chessmen.
All Scotland waits for her:
In the dark glens, beside the pale-green lochs
Men long for news.

Letters of thanks, letters from banks,
Letters of joy from girl and boy,
Receipted bills and invitations
To inspect new stock or visit relations,
And applications for situations
And timid lovers' declarations
And gossip, gossip from all the nations,
News circumstantial, news financial.
Letters with holiday snaps to enlarge in,
Letters with faces scrawled in the margin,
Letters from uncles, cousins and aunts,
Letters to Scotland from the South of France,
Letters of condolence to Highlands and Lowlands,
Notes from overseas to Hebrides –

Written on paper of every hue,
The pink, the violet, the white and the blue,
The chatty, the catty, the boring, adoring,
The cold and official and the heart's outpouring,
Clever, stupid, short and long,
The typed and the printed and the spelt all wrong.
Thousands are still asleep
Dreaming of terrifying monsters,
Of a friendly tea beside the band at Cranston's or Crawford's:
Asleep in working Glasgow, asleep in well-set Edinburgh,
Asleep in granite Aberdeen.
They continue their dreams;
But shall wake soon and long for letters,
And none will hear the postman's knock
Without a quickening of the heart,
For who can hear and feel himself forgotten?

W. H. Auden (1907–1973)

If the Earth Should Fall Tonight

If this little world tonight
Suddenly should fall through space
In a hissing, headlong flight,
Shrivelling from off its face,
As it falls into the sun
In an instant every trace
Of the little crawling things –
Ants, philosophers, and lice,
Cattle, cockroaches, and kings,
Beggars, millionaires and mice,
Men and maggots all as one
As it falls into the sun . . .
Who can say but at the same
Instant from some planet far,
A child may watch us and exclaim:
See the pretty shooting star.

Oliver Herford (1863–1935)

Poetry Jump-up

Tell me if Ah seeing right
Take a look down de street

Words dancin
words dancin
till dey sweat
words like fishes
jumpin out a net
words wild and free
joinin de poetry revelry
words back to back
words belly to belly

'Come on everybody
come and join de poetry band
dis is poetry carnival
dis is poetry bacchanal
when inspiration call
take yu pen in yu hand
if yu don't have a pen
take yu pencil in yu hand
if yu don't have a pencil
what the hell
so long as de feeling start to swell
just shout de poem out

Words jumpin off de page
tell me if Ah seein right
words like birds
jumpin out a cage
take a look down de street

Words shakin dey waist
words shaking dey bum
words wit black skin
words wit white skin
words wit brown skin
words wit no skin at all
words huggin up words
an sayin I want to be a poem today
rhyme or no rhyme
I is a poem today
I mean to have a good time

Words feeling hot hot hot
big words feelin hot hot hot
lil words feelin hot hot hot
even sad words cant help
tappin dey toe
to de riddum of de poetry band

Dis is poetry carnival
dis is poetry bacchanal
so come on everybody
join de celebration
all yu need is plenty perspiration
an a little inspiration
plenty perspiration
an a little inspiration

John Agard (1949–)

The Wraggle Taggle Gypsies

There were three gypsies a-come to my door,
And down-stairs ran this lady, O!
One sang high, and another sang low,
And the other sang, Bonny, bonny, Biscay, O!

Then she pulled off her silk finished gown
And put on hose of leather, O!
The ragged, ragged rags about our door –
She's gone with the wraggle taggle gypsies, O!

It was late last night, when my lord came home,
Enquiring for his a-lady, O!
The servants said on every hand:
'She's gone with the wraggle taggle gypsies, O!'

'O saddle to me my milk-white steed,
Go and fetch me my pony, O!
That I may ride and seek my bride,
Who is gone with the wraggle taggle gypsies, O!'

O he rode high and he rode low,
He rode through woods and copses too,
Until he came to an open field,
And there he espied his a-lady, O!

'What makes you leave your house and land?
What makes you leave your money, O?
What makes you leave your new-wedded lord;
To go with the wraggle taggle gypsies, O?'

'What care I for my house and my land?
What care I for my money, O?
What care I for my new-wedded lord?
I'm off with the wraggle taggle gypsies, O!'

'Last night you slept on a goose-feather bed,
With the sheet turned down so bravely, O!
And to-night you'll sleep in a cold open field,
Along with the wraggle taggle gypsies, O!'

'What care I for a goose-feather bed,
With the sheet turned down so bravely, O!
For to-night I shall sleep in a cold open field,
Along with the wraggle taggle gypsies, O!'

Anon.

Some One

Some one came knocking
At my wee, small door;
Some one came knocking,
I'm sure – sure – sure;
I listened, I opened,
I looked to left and right,
But nought there was a-stirring
In the still dark night;
Only the busy beetle
Tap-tapping in the wall,
Only from the forest
The screech-owl's call,
Only the cricket whistling
While the dewdrops fall,
So I know not who came knocking,
At all, at all, at all.

Walter de la Mare (1873–1956)

'There was an Old Man...'

There was an Old Man with a beard,
Who said, 'It is just as I feared! –
  Two Owls and a Hen,
  four Larks and a Wren,
Have all built their nests in my beard!'

Edward Lear (1812–1888)

Please Mrs Butler

Please Mrs Butler
This boy Derek Drew
Keeps copying my work, Miss.
What shall I do?

Go and sit in the hall, dear.
Go and sit in the sink.
Take your books on the roof,
   my lamb.
Do whatever you think.

Please Mrs Butler
This boy Derek Drew
Keeps taking my rubber, Miss.
What shall I do?

Keep it in your hand, dear.
Hide it up your vest.
Swallow it if you like, my love.
Do what you think best.

Please Mrs Butler
This boy Derek Drew
Keeps calling me rude names, Miss.
What shall I do?

Lock yourself in the cupboard, dear.
Run away to sea.
Do whatever you can, my flower.
But don't ask me!

Allan Allberg (1938–)

Sergeant Brown's Parrot

Many policemen wear upon their shoulders
Cunning little radios. To pass away the time
They talk about the traffic to them, listen to the news,
And it helps them to Keep Down Crime.

But Sergeant Brown, he wears upon his shoulder
A tall green parrot as he's walking up and down
And all the parrot says is 'Who's-a-pretty-boy-then?'
'I am,' says Sergeant Brown.

Kit Wright (1944–)

GOOD NIGHT

'Sunset and evening star'

Crossing the Bar

Sunset and evening star,
And one clear call for me.
And may there be no moaning of the bar,
When I put out to sea,

But such a tide as moving seems asleep,
Too full for sound and foam,
When that which drew from out the boundless deep
Turns again home.

Twilight and evening bell,
And after that the dark:
And may there be no sadness of farewell,
When I embark;

For tho' from out our bourne of Time and Place
The flood may bear me far,
I hope to see my Pilot face to face,
When I have crost the bar.

Alfred, Lord Tennyson (1809–1892)

Bilbo's Bath Song

Sing hey! for the bath at close of day
that washes the weary mud away!
A loon is he that will not sing:
O! Water Hot is a noble thing!

O! Sweet is the sound of falling rain,
and the brook that leaps from hill to plain:
but better than rain or rippling streams
is Water Hot that smokes and steams.

O! Water cold we may pour at need
down a thirsty throat and be glad indeed;
but better is Beer, if drink we lack,
and Water Hot poured down the back.

O! Water is fair that leaps on high
in a fountain white beneath the sky;
but never did fountain sound so sweet
as splashing Hot Water with my feet!

J. R. R. Tolkein (1892–1973)

Oranges and Lemons

Gay go up and gay go down,
To ring the bells of London town.

Oranges and lemons,
Say the bells of St. Clement's.

Brickbats and tiles,
Say the bells of St. Giles'.

Halfpence and farthings,
Say the bells of St. Martin's.

Pancakes and fritters,
Say the bells of St. Peter's.

Two sticks and an apple,
Say the bells at Whitechapel.

Old Father Baldpate,
Say the slow bells at Aldgate.

You owe me ten shillings,
Say the bells at St. Helen's.

Pokers and tongs,
Say the bells at St. John's.

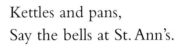

Kettles and pans,
Say the bells at St. Ann's.

When will you pay me?
Say the bells at Old Bailey.

When I grow rich,
Say the bells at Shoreditch.

Pray when will that be?
Say the bells of Stepney.

I am sure I don't know,
Says the great bell at Bow.

Here comes a candle to light you to bed,
And here comes a chopper to chop off your head.
Last, last, last, last, last man's head.

Anon.

Wynken, Blynken, and Nod

Wynken, Blynken, and Nod one night
Sailed off in a wooden shoe –
Sailed on a river of crystal light,
Into a sea of dew.
'Where are you going and what do you wish?'
The old moon asked the three.
'We have come to fish for the herring-fish
That live in this beautiful sea;
Nets of silver and gold have we,'
Said Wynken, Blynken, and Nod.

The old moon laughed and sang a song,
As they rocked in the wooden shoe,
And the wind that sped them all night long
Ruffled the waves of dew.
The little stars were the herring-fish
That lived in that beautiful sea –
'Now cast your nets wherever you wish –
But never afeared are we';
So cried the stars to the fishermen three:
Wyken, Blynken, and Nod.

All night long their nets
   they threw
To the stars in the
   twinkling foam –
Then down from the skies
   came the wooden shoe,
Bringing the fishermen home;
'Twas all so pretty a sail, it seemed
As if it could not be,
And some folks thought 'twas a dream they'd dreamed
Of sailing the beautiful sea –
But I shall name you the fishermen three:
Wynken, Blynken, and Nod.

Wynken and Blynken are two little eyes,
And Nod is a little head,
And the wooden shoe that sailed the skies
Is a wee one's trundle-bed.
So shut your eyes while mother sings
Of wonderful sights that be,
And you shall see the beautiful things
As you rock on the misty sea,
Where the old shoe rocked the fishermen three:
Wynken, Blynken, and Nod.

Eugene Field (1850–1895)

Prayer at Bedtime

Matthew, Mark, Luke, and John
Bless the bed that I lie on.
Before I lay me down to sleep,
I pray the Lord my soul to keep.

Four corners to my bed,
Four angels there are spread;
Two at the foot, two at the head:
Four to carry me when I'm dead.

I go by sea, I go by land:
The Lord made me with His right hand.
Should any danger come to me,
Sweet Jesus Christ deliver me.

He's the branch and I'm the flower,
Pray God send me a happy hour;
And should I die before I wake,
I pray the Lord my soul to take.

Anon.

Farewell

Thy journey be auspicious; may the breeze,
Gentle and soothing, fan thy cheek; may lakes
All bright with lily cups delight thine eye,
The sunbeam's heat be cooled by shady trees,
The dust beneath thy feet the pollen be
Of lotuses.

From a Sanskrit play c. 400 AD

'You spotted snakes'

(extract from A Midsummer-Night's Dream)

You spotted snakes with double tongue,
    Thorny hedge-hogs, be not seen;
Newts, and blind-worms, do no wrong;
    Come not near our fairy queen.

      Philomel, with melody,
      Sing in our sweet lullaby;
Lulla, lulla, lullaby; lulla, lulla, lullaby:
      Never harm,
      Nor spell, nor charm,
      Come our lovely lady nigh;
      So, good night, with lullaby.

Weaving spiders come not here;
    Hence, you long-legg'd spinners, hence!
Beetles black, approach not near;
    Worm nor snail, do no offence.

      Philomel, with melody,
      Sing in our sweet lullaby;
Lulla, lulla, lullaby; lulla, lulla, lullaby:
      Never harm,
      Nor spell, nor charm,
      Come our lovely lady nigh;
      So, good night, with lullaby.

      William Shakespeare (1564–1616)

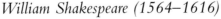

Auld Lang Syne

Should auld acquaintance be forgot,
And never brought to min'?
Should auld acquaintance be forgot,
And auld lang syne?

> *For auld lang syne, my dear.*
> *For auld lang syne,*
> *We'll tak a cup o' kindness yet,*
> *For auld lang syne.*

We twa hae run about the braes,
And pu'd the gowans† fine;   †daisies
But we've wandered mony a weary foot
Sin' auld lang syne.
We twa hae paidled i' the burn,
From morning sun till dine;
But seas between us braid hae roared
Sin' auld lang syne.

And there's a hand, my trusty fiere,[†]   [†]comrade
And gie's a hand o' thine;
And we'll tak a right guid-willie waught,[†]   [†]drink
For auld lang syne.

And surely ye'll be your pint-stowp,
And surely I'll be mine;
And we'll tak a cup o' kindness yet
For auld lang syne.

> *For auld lang syne, my dear.*
> *For auld lang syne,*
> *We'll tak a cup o' kindness yet,*
> *For auld lang syne.*

Robert Burns
(1759–1776)

'God be in my head'

God be in my head
  And in my understanding;
God be in my eyes
  And in my looking;
God be in my mouth,
  And in my speaking;
God be in my heart,
  And in my thinking;
God be at mine end,
  And at my departing.

Anon.

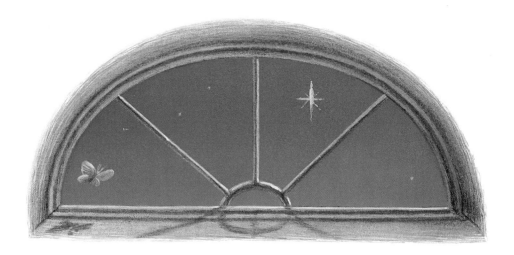

The Star

Twinkle, twinkle, little star,
How I wonder what you are!
Up above the world so high,
Like a diamond in the sky.

When the blazing sun is gone,
When he nothing shines upon,
Then you show your little light,
Twinkle, twinkle, all the night.

Then the traveller in the dark,
Thanks you for your tiny spark,
He could not see which way to go,
If you did not twinkle so.

In the dark blue sky you keep,
And often through my curtains peep,
For you never shut your eye,
Till the sun is in the sky.

As your bright and tiny spark,
Lights the traveller in the dark –
Though I know not what you are,
Twinkle, twinkle, little star.

Jane Tayler (1783–1824)

'Twinkle, twinkle, little bat'

Twinkle, twinkle, little bat!
How I wonder what you're at!
Up above the world you fly,
Like a tea-tray in the sky.

Lewis Carroll (1832–1898)

The White Seal's Lullaby

Oh! hush thee, my baby, the night is behind us,
And black are the waters that sparkled so green.
The moon, o'er the combers, looks downward to find us
At rest in the hollows that rustle between.

Where billow meets billow, there soft be thy pillow;
Ah, weary wee flipperling, curl at thy ease!
The storm shall not wake thee, nor sharks overtake thee,
Asleep in the arms of the slow-swinging seas.

Rudyard Kipling (1865–1936)

Stopping by Woods on a Snowy Evening

Whose woods these are I think I know.
His house is in the village, though;
He will not see me stopping here
To watch his woods fill up with snow.

My little horse must think it queer
To stop without a farmhouse near
Between the woods and frozen lake
The darkest evening of the year.

He gives his harness bells a shake
To ask if there is some mistake
The only other sound's the sweep
Of easy wind and downy flake

The woods are lovely, dark, and deep,
But I have promises to keep,
And miles to go before I sleep,
And miles to go before I sleep.

Robert Frost (1874–1963)

A Cradle Song

Golden slumbers kiss your eyes,
Smiles awake you when you rise.
Sleep, pretty wantons, do not cry,
And I will sing a lullaby:
Rock them, rock them, lullaby.

Care is heavy, therefore sleep you;
You are care, and care must keep you.
Sleep, pretty wantons, do not cry,
And I will sing a lullaby:
Rock them, rock them, lullaby.

Thomas Dekker (1572–1632)

'When that I was and a little tiny boy'
(extract from Twelfth Night)

When that I was and a little tiny boy,
    With hey, ho, the wind and the rain;
A foolish thing was but a toy,
    For the rain it raineth every day.

But when I came to man's estate,
    With hey, ho, the wind and the rain;
'Gainst knaves and thieves men shut their gates,
    For the rain it raineth every day.

But when I came, alas! to wive,
    With hey, ho, the wind and the rain;
By swaggering could I never thrive,
    For the rain it raineth every day.

But when I came unto my beds,
    With hey, ho, the wind and the rain;
With toss-pots still had drunken heads,
    For the rain it raineth every day.

A great while ago the world begun,
    With hey, ho, the wind and the rain;
But that's all one, our play is done,
    And we'll strive to please you every day.

William Shakespeare (1564–1616)

INDEX OF POEMS

INDEX OF FIRST LINES

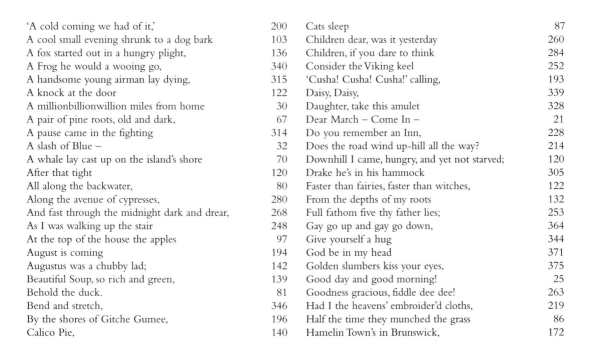

INDEX OF POETS

ACKNOWLEDGEMENTS

The publishers wish to thank the following for permission to use copyright material:

John Agard, 'Poetry Jump Up' from *Get Back Pimple* published by Viking 1996, by permission of the Caroline Sheldon Literary Agency; **Allan Ahlberg,** 'Please Mrs Butler' from *Please Mrs Butler:* Verses, Kestrel Books, 1983, copyright © Allan Ahlberg 1983, by permission of Penguin UK; **W H Auden,** 'Over the heather the wet wind blows' and 'Night Mail' from *Collected Poems,* by permission of Faber and Faber Ltd; **Hilaire Belloc,** 'Matilda' and 'Tarantella' from *Complete Verse,* Random House, by permission of The Peters Fraser and Dunlop Group Ltd on behalf of the Estate of the author; **Sir John Betjeman,** an extract from *Summoned by Bells,* by permission of John Murray (Publishers) Ltd; **Alan Brownjohn,** 'We are going to see the rabbit', copyright © 1983, 1988, by permission of Rosica Colin Ltd on behalf of the author; **Charles Causley,** 'Leonardo' from *All Day Saturday,* 'Timothy Winters', 'The Reverend Sabine Baring-Gould' and 'I Saw a Jolly Hunter' from *Figgie Hobbin* by permission of David Higham Assoc; **G K Chesterton,** 'The Donkey' and an extract from 'Lepanto', by permission of A P Watt on behalf of The Royal Literary Fund; **Wendy Cope,** 'Kindness to Animals' from *Serious Concerns,* by permission of Faber and Faber Ltd; **E E Cummings,** 'maggie and milly and molly and may', 'now is a ship' and 'in Just-' from *Complete Poems 1904-62,* ed. George J Firmage, copyright © 1991 by the Trustees for the E E Cummings Trust and George James Firmage, by permission of W W Norton & Company Ltd; **John Drinkwater,** 'Moonlit Apples', by permission of Samuel French Ltd on behalf of the Estate of the author; **Richard Edwards,** 'Oh, To Be...' and 'Aerobics' from *There's a Mouse in my Roof,* by permission of Orchard Books, a division of the Watts Publishing Group; **T S Eliot,** 'Journey of the Magi' and 'Macavity: the Mystery Cat' from *The Complete Poems and Plays,* by permission of Faber and Faber Ltd; **Eleanor Farjeon,** 'Cats', 'Mrs Malone' and 'Tide in the River' from *Silver Sand and Snow,* Michael Joseph, by permission of David Higham Associates on behalf of the Estate of the author; **Max Fatchen,** 'Isn't it Amazing?' from *Peculiar Rhymes and Lunatic Lines,* by permission of Orchard Books, a division of the Watts Publishing Group; **Rachel Field,** 'Something Told the Wild Geese' from *Poems,* Macmillan, New York, 1957, by permission of Simon & Schuster Books for Young Readers, an imprint of Simon & Schuster Children's Publishing Division; **Robert Frost,** 'Stopping by Woods on a Snowy Evening' from *The Poetry of Robert Frost,* ed. Edward Connery Lathem, Jonathan Cape, copyright © 1923, 1969 by Henry Holt and Co, copyright © 1951 by Robert Frost, by permission of Random House UK and Henry Holt & Co, Inc; **John Galsworthy,** 'Never Get Out', by permission of The Society of Authors as the literary representative of the Estate of the author; **Carmen Bernos de Gasztold,** 'The Prayer of the Cat' and 'The Prayer of the Foal' from *Prayers from the Ark,* trans. Rumer Godden, 1963, by permission of Macmillan Children's Books and Curtis Brown on behalf of the Estate of the author; **Stella Gibbons,** 'Lullaby for a Baby Toad' from *The Mountain Beast and Other Poems,* copyright © 1950 Stella Gibbons, by permission of Curtis Brown Ltd on behalf of the Estate of the author; **Nikki Giovanni,** 'poem for ntombi iayo (at five weeks of age)' from *Spin a Soft Black Song,* copyright © 1971, 1985 by Nikki Giovanni, by permission of Hill and Wang, a division of Farrar, Straus & Giroux, Inc; **Kenneth Grahame,** 'Duck's Ditty' from *The Wind in the Willows,* copyright © The University Chest, Oxford, by permission of Curtis Brown Ltd on behalf of The University Chest, Oxford; **Robert Graves,** 'Vain and Careless' and 'Warning to Children' from *Complete Poems,* by permission of Carcanet Press and Oxford University Press, Inc; **Thomas Hardy,** 'The Fallow Deer at the Lonely House' from *The Complete Poems by Thomas Hardy,* ed. James Gibson, Papermac, by permission of Macmillan General Books; **Seamus Heaney,** 'Blackberry Picking', 'The Railway Children' and 'Mid-Term Break' from *New Selected Poems 1966-1987,* by permission of Faber and Faber; **Adrian Henri,** 'Any Prince to Any Princess' in *Collected Poems,* Allison and Busby, 1986, copyright © Adrian Henri 1986, by permission of Rogers, Coleridge and White Ltd on behalf of the author; **A D Hope,** 'Tiger' from *Collected Poems,* by permission of HarperCollins Publishers, Australia; **A E Housman,** 'The African Lion', by permission of The Society of Authors as the literary representative of the Estate of the author; **Ted Hughes,** 'The Horses' from *New Selected Poems 1957-1994,* copyright © 1957 by Ted Hughes, and 'Full Moon and Little Frieda' from *New Selected Poems 1957-1994,* copyright © 1972 by Ted Hughes by permission of Faber & Faber Ltd; **Elizabeth Jennings,** 'The Ark' from *The Secret Brother,* 'The Riding School' from *After the Ark* OUP 1978 by permission of David Higham Assoc; **Jenny Joseph,** 'Warning' from *Selected Poems,* Bloodaxe Books Ltd, copyright © Jenny Joseph 1992, by permission of John Johnson Ltd on behalf of the author; **Rudyard Kipling,** 'If', 'The Hump', 'The White Seal's Lullaby' and 'A Smuggler's Song', by permission of A P Watt Ltd on behalf of The National Trust; **James Kirkup,** 'The Lonely Scarecrow' from *Refusal to Conform,* Oxford University Press, 1963, by permission of the author; **D H Lawrence,** 'Humming-Bird', 'Giorno Dei Morte' and 'Piano' from *The Complete Poems of D H Lawrence,* ed. V de Sola Pinto and F W Roberts, copyright © 1964, 1971 by Angelo Ravagli and C M Weekley, Executors of the Estate of Frieda Lawrence Ravagli, by permission of Laurence Pollinger Ltd on behalf of the Estate of Frieda Lawrence Ravagli and Viking Penguin, a division of Penguin Books USA Inc; **Dennis Lee,** 'Lizzie's Lion', by permission of Stoddart Publishing Co Ltd, Canada; **C S Lewis,** 'The Late Passenger' from *Poems, 1964,* ed. Walter Hooper, copyright © 1964 by the Executors of the Estate of C S Lewis and renewed 1992 by C S Lewis Pte Ltd and Walter Hooper, by permission of HarperCollins Publishers Ltd and Harcourt Brace and Company; **George Macbeth,** 'The Burmese Cats' from *Poems of Love and Death,* Martin Secker & Warburg, 1980, copyright © 1980 George Macbeth by permission of Reed Consumer Books Ltd and Scribner, a division of Simon and Schuster; **Brian McCabe,** 'Tree' from

Island of the Children, Orchard Books, by permission of the author; **Roger McGough**, 'First Day at School' from *In the Glassroom*, Jonathan Cape, and 'No Peas For The Wicked', by permission of The Peters Fraser and Dunlop Group Ltd on behalf of the author; **Ian McMillan**, 'Names Of Scottish Islands To Be Shouted In A Bus Queue When You Are Feeling Bored' by permission of the author; **Colin McNaughton**, 'Mum's Having A Baby' copyright © Colin McNaughton 1990 from *Who's Been Sleeping In My Porridge* and 'The Garden's Full Of Witches' copyright © Colin McNaughton 1987, from *There's An Awful Lot Of Weirdos In Our Neighbourhood* by permission of Walker Books Ltd; **Margaret Mahy**, 'Goodness Gracious!' from *The First Margaret Mahy Story Book*, J M Dent, by permission of Orion Publishing Group Ltd; **Walter de la Mare**, 'The Listeners', 'King David' and 'Some One' from *The Complete Poems of Walter de la Mare*, 1969, by permission of the Literary Trustees of the author and The Society of Authors as their representative; **John Masefield**, 'Cargoes', by permission of The Society of Authors as the literary representative of the Estate of the author; **Eve Merriam**, 'Thumbprint' from *A Sky Full of Poems*, copyright © 1964, 1970, 1973, 1986 by Eve Merriam, renewed 1992 by Eve Merriam, by permission of Marian Reiner on behalf of the Estate of the author; **Edna St Vincent Millay**, 'Counting-out Rhyme', copyright © The Estate of the late Edna St Vincent Millay, by permission of A M Heath on behalf of the Estate of the author; **A A Milne**, 'Disobedience' and 'The King's Breakfast' from *When We Were Very Young*, Methuen Children's Books, copyright © 1924 by E P Dutton, renewed 1952 by A A Milne, by permission of Reed Consumer Books Ltd and Dutton Children's Books, a division of Penguin Books USA Inc; **Adrian Mitchell**, 'Not a Very Cheerful Song, I'm Afraid' from *Balloon Lagoon* (1997), by permission of The Peters Fraser and Dunlop Group Ltd on behalf of the author, copyright © 1984 Adrian Mitchell. Adrian Mitchell asks that none of his poems are used in connection with any examinations whatsoever; **John Mole**, 'Moth' from *The Mad Parrot's Countdown*, copyright © John Mole 1990, by permission of Peterloo Poets; **Edwin Morgan**, 'The Loch Ness Monster's Song' from *Collected Poems*, by permission of Carcanet Press Ltd; **Brian Morse**, 'Crack-a-Dawn' from *Picnic on the Moon*, 1990, by permission of Turton & Chambers Ltd; **Ogden Nash**, 'The Duck' from *The Ogden Nash Pocket Book*, Pocket Books, copyright © 1944 by Ogden Nash, renewed, by permission of Curtis Brown, Ltd on behalf of the Estate of the author and Little Brown and Company; **Henry Newbolt**, 'Drake's Drum' from *Selected Poems of Henry Newbolt*, Hodder & Stoughton, 1981, by permission of Peter Newbolt; **Grace Nichols**, 'Give Yourself A Hug' from *Give Yourself a Hug*, copyright © Grace Nichols 1994 by permission of Curtis Brown Group Ltd; **Alfred Noyes**, 'The Highwayman' from *Collected Poems*, by permission of John Murray (Publishers) Ltd; **Brian Patten**, 'You Can't Be That' and 'The Pet Wig' from *Thawing Frozen Frogs*, Puffin, 1990, copyright © Brian Patten 1990, and 'A Small Dragon' from *Notes to the Hurrying Man*, Allen & Unwin, 1969, copyright © Brian Patten 1969, by permission of Rogers, Coleridge and White on behalf of the author; **Sylvia Plath**, 'Mushrooms' from *Collected Poems*, by permission of Faber & Faber Ltd; **James Reeves**, 'Cows', 'Beech Leaves' and 'Grim and Gloomy' from *Complete Poems for Children*, Heinemann, by permission of Laura Cecil Literary Agency on behalf of the Estate of the author; **E V Rieu**, 'Lullaby for a Naughty Girl', by permission of D C H Rieu, Executor of the Estate of the author; **Michael Rosen**, 'Me and My Brother', from *The Hypnotiser*, Andre Deutsch Children's Books, an imprint of Scholastic Children's Books, copyright ©1988 Michael Rosen, by permission of Scholastic Ltd; **Ian Serraillier**, 'Anne and the Field-Mouse' from *Happily Ever After*, Oxford University Press, 1963, by permission of Anne Serraillier; **Shel Silverstein**, 'The Little Boy and the Old Man' from *A Light in the Attic*, copyright © 1981 by Evil Eye Music, Inc, by permission of Edite Kroll Literary Agency on behalf of the author and HarperCollins Publishers, Inc; **Sir John Squire**, 'There was an Indian', by permission of Raglan Squire; **L A G Strong**, 'Lowery Cot' from *The Body's Imperfections*, by permission of The Peters Fraser and Dunlop Group Ltd on behalf of the Estate of the author; **Matthew Sweeney**, 'Cows on the Beach' from *The Flying Spring Onion*, by permission of Faber and Faber Ltd; **D M Thomas**, 'Whale' from *Selected Poems*, Martin Secker & Warburg, 1983, by permission of John Johnson Ltd on behalf of the Estate of the author; **R S Thomas**, 'Tramp' from *Collected Poems 1945-1990*, J M Dent, by permission of Orion Publishing Group Ltd; **J R R Tolkien**, 'Bilbo's Bath Song' from *Lord of the Rings*, by permission of HarperCollins Publishers; **Williams Carlos Williams**, 'This is just to say' from Collected Poems 1909-1939, copyright © 1938 by New Directions Publishing Corp, by permission of Carcanet Press Ltd and New Directions Publishing Corp; **Valerie Worth**, 'barefoot' from *Still More Small Poems*, copyright © 1976, 1977, 1978 by Valerie Worth, by permission of Farrar, Straus & Giroux, Inc; **Kit Wright**, 'Sergeant Brown's Parrot' and 'Watch Your French' from *Rabbiting On* copyright © Kit Wright 1978 by permission of the author; **W B Yeats**, 'Aedh Wishes for the Cloths of Heaven' and 'The Song of the Wandering Aengus' from *The Collected Poems of W B Yeats*, Vol. I: The Poems, revised and edited by Richard J Finneran, copyright © 1983, 1989 by Anne Yeats, by permission of A P Watt on behalf of Michael Yeats and Simon & Schuster, and 'The Cat and the Moon' from *The Collected Poems of W B Yeats*, by permission of A P Watt on behalf of Michael Yeats.

Every effort has been made to trace the copyright holders but if any have been inadvertently overlooked the publishers will be pleased to make the necessary arrangement at the first opportunity.